F

Chapter 1

It was September 8th, 1972, a Saturday. That afternoon, an ambulance was seen going along 13th Street with its siren blaring. It split off to Lake Road. Shortly after, the same ambulance turned around and returned in the opposite direction.

It joined 13th Street and headed back in the direction from which it had originally come from. People watched it as it rose and descended the slope of an elevated bridge built to allow for the passing of the rail line below it. With time only the echo of the siren came through and it gradually faded away until it was completely gone.

The ambulance arrived at the New Orleans medical facility ten minutes later. Potters at the emergency room sprinted outside to welcome the recently arrived outpatient. The ambulance driver emerged from the vehicle, walked to the back and opened the rear doors. With assistance from two male potters, the ambulance attendants leapt from the vehicle. The legs unfurled and the wheels touched the ground as soon as the bed was fully removed from the ambulance. The hospital's entrance was open and the bed was shoved through.

Ruth exhaled and uttered, *"woo...woo. Pooh...pooh."*
Hold on, honey, you're safe now. We're at the hospital. "Trying to let his wife know where she was," Richard remarked.

"Please, where would I find a phone? I need to make some calls." Richard asked the nurse, who was busy reassuring Ruth that everything would be okay.

Richard was not a stranger at the hospital in New Orleans, so it was an odd question for him to ask. He had visited the hospital several times before, including during the delivery of his first-born son, so he was extremely familiar with its layout. Who would, however, dispute his mental state. Few people would be as alert and capable of managing themselves in such situations as he was. Without ever looking away from her patient, the nurse responded, *"over there,"* pointing to the registry and then added, *"and please go to the waiting room when you are done."* It had more of a commanding tone than anything else.

She continued, *"I'll come to update you on the progress,"* as they stopped in front of the elevator doors and she hit the elevator button.

Richard looked on as his wife was pushed inside the

elevator and finally, swallowed up. He ran his left arm across his forehead and his shirtsleeve wiped the drops of sweat that had collected across it.

The public phone was mounted on the wall just opposite the registry. He was by the phone in a minute, making calls to his parents and in-laws. He entered some digits on the phone's dial pad.

"Hello this is the operator, what can I do for you?" A voice came through the earpiece after three rings.

"Hello, this is Richard Wright calling from New Orleans Medical Centre. I would like to make a reverse Call to 1- 130-311-2470."

"Who is the owner of this line and who would you like to talk to?" asked the operator.

"It's a residential line and I'd like to talk to my parents,"

Richard answered. The operator urged him to hold on. Temporarily, the line went silent. Shortly, he heard buzzes and clicks, then a voice came through. It was his mother.

"Hello... Hello mum, it's Richard, we are at the hospital."

"Yes, what's wrong, is it Ruth again?"

Richard could hear the anxiety in his mother's voice.

"Yes, its Ruth and I think this time She's going to have a baby, but please

don't panic."

"Oh my God, when did that start?" She asked.

"About two hours ago," Richard answered.

"Richard, why didn't you call sooner? Come on you don't take chances with a pregnancy."

"It's alright mother, we thought it'd stop just like the last time."

"Let me call your father and we will be there shortly."

Richard hung up when the line went dead but picked it up right away. He made another call, this time to his in-laws, using the identical call setup. Richard recognized the baritone voice at the other end of this call as the response came through.

"Hello! sorry for the reverse call but the phone cards are out. This is Richard calling from the hospital."

Richard thought it was best to clear the old man's mind just in case he would have questions as to why he had placed a reverse call.

"There has to be a reason for it, I know that, Richard, there is no need to apologize, and you have done well."

His father in-law sounded very pleasant and that took a lot of uneasiness out of his voice.

"So, Richard, is something wrong?" His father-in law

asked him.

Richard took a moment to figure out how best to put it. His father in-law got a shiver down his spine during the brief period of silence. Richard didn't want to convey a particularly ominous message, not realizing that his brief silence had already done so.

"Not really," he finally managed to say and thought that was a fair answer.

"We have just got here, and Ruth is about to have a baby," he went on and precisely put it across.

"So, how's she doing?" The old man inquired.

In the kitchen, Mrs. Wilson was an eaves dropping on the conversation her husband was having with the person on the phone. Initially, she had not paid much attention when the call just came, but as her husband went on talking, she felt compelled to pay closer attention. She needed confirmation, but from what she could make out, she believed it was Richard was on the other end of the phone.

Making her way from the stove to the kitchen door and through the hall, she shouted her question to her husband, *"Peter! Who's on the line?"*

Mr. Wilson put his left hand over the phone's mouthpiece and lowered his right arm from the side of his head. *"It's Richard,"* Mr. Wilson answered back on top of his voice.

Mrs. Wilson rushed to the living room as soon as her assumption was confirmed.

"Let me talk to him," She requested. Mr. Wilson kept his silence. He was listening to what Richard was saying.

"Let me talk to him," she insisted but Mr. Wilson kept on listening.

"They have taken her to the delivery room and I'm yet to be briefed. Anyway, don't worry, she is fine, and I will call you back as soon as I know anything," Richard said.

"Please do, your mother is here, I'm sure she won't move away from this phone until she hears from you."

"Let me talk to him," Mrs Wilson insisted even further.

At her last appeal, Mr. Wilson put back the handset on the receiver. *"Peter,"* Mrs Wilson called her husband by his first name as usual.

"How could you do that? You heard me request to talk to him." Mrs. Wilson took her husband to task.

The Virtues of Split Personality

"You and your conversations, what did you want me to do? I don't think he has the time. The boy just said bye. Why can't you be patient and wait? Talk to him when he calls back."

"And when is that going to be?" Mrs. Wilson retorted.

"He has promised to do so when he knows something, as for now, she is in the theatre," Mr. Wilson revealed to his wife and tried to reason with her.

"Well, you could have asked him to call Rabecca then, I'm sure, she would have loved to be by Ruth's side."

"Susan, why can't you call her yourself?" He called his wife by her first name too.

Mr. Wilson furiously responded, making it clear that his wife was making irrational charges and that her demands were unreasonable.

"And what did you mean by me and my conversations? I just wanted to hear how she is doing."

"Susan, I know you. I don't understand why you should be so insistent on talking to him; you just wanted to talk, right? To ask about the same things he has already told me. So, feel free to ask me if you genuinely want to know."

Mrs. Wilson fell silent, and her husband gave her a long,

scornful stare.

"I thought so. I believe I have told you all you need to know," Mr. Wilson said.

After Richard had hang the phone he walked to the waiting room, found himself a seat and sat down. For a while, he was patient but as the waiting continued, he could not stand it any longer, anxiety was killing him. He got up from the seat and began to pace back and forth from one end of the room to other. The nurse had not kept her promise, and he hoped and prayed there would no complications. A while later, his parents walked into the room. His mother raced toward him and gave him a hug.

"How is she?" She asked him. Before he could answer her question, his father also asked.

"Yes, any news?" Mr Wilson asked as he shook his son's hand.

"Not yet," Richard answered.

"God, these people, what is going on here, do they know what it feels like to wait like this? Anything can happen in there and we deserve to know every step of the way."

Mr. Wright continued, hysterically lamenting the hospital staff's lack of consideration. Amid his speech he noticed some people in the room had their looks past him to the other side of the room.

His mouth stuck open wide, he turned and looked behind him in the direction of the door. The Doctor had walked in still in his theatre clothes. Had it not been for the doctor's sudden entry into the room, Mr. Wright could have probably gone on and on talking.

Just as the doctor entered through the double-flapping door, all eyes in the room focused on him. His abrupt arrival in the room broke a lot of anxiety but only that of the Wright's family were ultimately relieved.

"Mr. Richard Wright," the doctor called out. Richard walked away from his father and mother, towards the doctor.

"Yes please," he responded.

"You are, Mr. Richard Wright?" Just to be sure the doctor asked, directing the question to the man who had walked, came and stood before him.

"Yes," Richard answered.

Positioning himself by Richard's side, Mr. Wright uttered, *"Doctor, you are just on time, we were wondering why no one has been assigned to brief us on the proceedings. We have been in suspense all this time."*

"You are...?" The doctor asked.

"Mr. Wright... Wright senior, this here is my son." Mr. Wright responded and touched Richard on the shoulder.

"I'm sorry about that. Anyway, it's fortunate she got here just on time for the staff to carry out the delivery procedure. However, something unexpected happened," the doctor added.

Richard's eyes shot out and his father immediately drew his face back, raising his thick, white brows. As he did so, parallel lines began to form around his intensely dark eyes, and the rest of his face developed ridges and furrows.

The final bit of information was hastily met with fear. The doctor instantly resumed his briefing after noticing the strain on their expressions.

"We were actually caught up in something we should have known long before we began the delivery procedure. Just after our successful first procedure. Ruth indicated to us that something else was happening. Immediately, we got to work again."

"What are you saying, did something go wrong?" Mr. Wright asked.

Turning to Richard, the doctor continued, "We were lucky everything went on well and I'm glad to say you are a father of two sons. Identical twins and their mother is just fine."

"Jesus, where are they?" Richard rushed out of the waiting area.

The doctor went after him. *"Richard! They are still being cleaned, you will need to wait for a while. Besides you cannot go in the theatre like that."*

"Why not?" Richard asked.

"You are not properly dressed; you can only be allowed if you are dressed as I am," the doctor said.

The doctor was dressed in the green scrubs (green slacks and a green short-sleeved top. His head covered in a headdress of the same colour.

"And do you know where the theatre is?" The doctor asked him. Richard shook his head from side to side.

"Anyway, that is beside the point," the doctor disapprovingly said, contradicting himself.

"Please go to room 103 on the third floor and wait for them, they'll be there in a few minutes. I'm sure they are almost done by now. Take the elevator just behind you."

Richard was so ecstatic that he left the room as if his family was already where he was heading. After punching the elevator button several times, the doors didn't open. The indicator light indicated that the elevator was located someplace on the upper floors. He could not wait. He ran to the flight of stairs. Midway the first set of stairs on his way up, he stumbled and landed on all fours. The fall did not slow him down; he hastily got himself up and continued the climb. Finally, he got to the room panting. They were not there yet and he wondered if he'd heard the doctor right. He took two steps back to take a look at the room number, 103.

'Yes, this is it, I certainly heard him right,' he reassured himself.

He paced back and forth as he waited, but it seemed like an eternity. He repeatedly dusted the bed, as though there was dust on it. Even without touching them, one could tell that the pillows were soft and appeared to be comfortable enough, yet he continued rearranging and smoothing them.

While he was still busy with his last few minutes' actions, the door opened, and a nurse backed in pulling a bed with his wife on it. Richard dashed and helped the nurse to position the bed and move his wife to the bed in the room. After that was done Richard was all over his wife.

"Ah...Ah, Mr. Wright, she is still tired, give her at least two hours... for now

The Virtues of Split Personality

let her rest. The babies are in the nursery for observation you can go and see them there,"

Richard kissed his wife on the forehead and ran out of the room.

Richard's parents were still in the waiting area unsure of what to do, as he had left them without a word with the doctor trailing right behind him.

"What on earth is wrong with him?" without directly addressing anyone, Mr. Wright asked.

"I don't comprehend, how he can just leave us in that manner. Don't tell me he has forgotten we've both been waiting here," Mr. Wright said while addressing his wife, in an effort to get a response from her.

"Don't act like you're not a father; you know the excitement of having a child. I'm sure he is surprised and just overwhelmed to hear that he has twins. He will come around and come back for us," Mrs. Wright said. *"Whatever the case, this is not his first time. I don't know about you, but I should be treated with respect. Were we not only criticizing the hospital staff for failing to inform us during the delivery?"* Mr. Wright replied, *"and he is doing exactly the same."*

"Excuse me. We're in a hospital I'm not going to go into those long arguments with you," his wife said and when he heard those

words; he knew that was the end of the conversation.

Richard suddenly remembered his parents as he was en-route to the nursery to see his newborn babies. He immediately made a U-turn and hurried down to the waiting area. When he arrived, he discovered that Rabecca, his wife's aunt, had also come.

"What were you thinking when you walked out on us just like that?" His father asked him.

Richard looked at him then turned to face his mother. He went silent briefly. He was trying to understand what it was that he had done wrong, to offend his father. *'Is that really offensive?'* Richard reflected. Somehow, he realized his father was simply being his usual critical self.

"I don't know what to say. Anyway, I'm sorry," he apologized. He knew an apology was the only thing that was going to bring that subsequent development to an end.

Turning to Rabecca, he exclaimed *"it's good to see you."*

"Good to see you too, Richard, and congratulations. I came as soon as I heard. Susan called me soon after you informed them."

"Let's all go and see the babies." With those words he gestured them to move as he led the way. *"I actually haven't seen them as*

well."

"*So, where the hell did you go?*" His father questioned.

"*I saw Ruth briefly and, on my way, to see the boys I remembered you and mum were still back here.*"

It was only when they got to the babies that Richard came to the realization that they were completely unprepared for their twins.

"What would you call them?" asked his father.

"*That had not crossed my mind until you asked. Anyway, it has to wait, because we were not expecting twins. We had two names one for a boy and the other for a girl, that is how prepared we were.*"

"What name did you have for a boy?"

"*Christopher, Christopher Wright,*" Richard responded.

Walking to the boys, Mr. Wright called out "*Christopher!*"

"*So, which one are you calling?*" It was Richard's turn to ask.

"*Both of them,*" his father answered.

Richard was awestruck. He intervened saying "*That is ludicrous and not conceivable.*" It was one of those rare occasions where

Richard felt like disagreeing with his father.

"As long as you are not breaking any law, I think it's worth the precedence. These boys look to me like identical twins, which makes it even more interesting. I would love to be part of their everyday lives and see what the future holds for them. Bear it in mind, with identical twins it's same everything. I rest my case just there."

"It's most likely illegal. Although I've never heard of what you are suggesting, I find your proposal intriguing and somewhat attractive. Although I don't believe Ruth would, I kind of like it.

"You can't afford to consult the legal books for every decision you make, and secondly, adventure is what makes life fascinating. About Ruth, you have to convince her, she is your wife, isn't she?" His father said re-enforcing his point.

"Of course she is," Richard responded.

"Then I don't see any problem," Mr. Wright said. An impression reminding his son that he was the head of his family and all he had to do was to rise up to it.

"Richard, don't listen to your father. These are your kids with Ruth and your father has nothing to do with it. You have to listen to her before you settle for such crazy ideas," his mother disapproved of her husband's intoxicating thinking and tried to reason with her son.

"If everyone was like you, life would be unbearably dull," Mr. Wright said, pointing at his wife, *"The problem with you is, you are too holy."*

"Because you get dangerously thrilled about practically anything, you believe I'm dead boring. I may seem very uninteresting to you, but I believe that I'm the best thing that has ever happened to you; without me, your life would have been very different. And if I am so dull, why are you still with me? Am sure there are a lot of interesting and excited women as you are, out there."

"Whatever, but don't forget I proposed to you and not the other way round, so, I chose my destiny." Mr. Wright said still trying to emerge a victor as always.

Just before she could hit back, Richard kicked in,

"Mother, I know you two can go on and on, just forget it. Let's go and see Ruth."

"No... No... No. Richard your father should learn to acknowledge that other people make things happen for him. It's not that I'm stupid; I have actually tolerated a lot of his irrational ideas and accepted him as he is. Tell me, is it wrong to be a good wife?" Her last statement was kind of directed to both her husband and son.

Grabbing his mother by her hand and leading her to see his wife, Richard softly said *"Mother let's go."*

The Virtues of Split Personality

His father and Juliet calmly followed the two of them behind. As soon as they got to Ruth, Juliet sauntered right to her. She couldn't hide her anxiety any longer.

"Hi Ruth, how are you doing?"

"Fine," Ruth responded weakly.

"I came as soon as I heard. We have just been to see the boys, they are beautiful. Did you know you were carrying twins?" Rabecca asked.

"Not in a day," she replied in an almost inaudible voice again.

Richard walked to his wife's side and ran her through his father's naming of the boys - suggestion.

"Jesus! Where on earth? That would be a problem differentiating them. For God' sake don't forget they are identical twins," Ruth said.

"It's fine with me because I think that is what makes it even more interesting. Well, you can name them; you have the right to do so if you don't like our idea."

Richard threw the weight of the subject and responsibility to his wife, but she was still weak to rise to the challenge.

Ruth remained quiet. Richard took a step backwards. *"Any suggestions?"* He asked his wife again, but she maintained her silence.

"Well, I take it you are okay with our decision."

With tired eyes she just looked at him and remained silent. Tired as she was, debating with him seemed boring.

The following morning Ruth and the twins got discharged. The twins' birth certificates were done. The names on the certificates were Christopher Wright on each. The system was so easy, thanks to the network between the hospital and the Ministry of home Affairs. The hospital was allowed to issue birth certificates because of the link, upon birth.

Chapter 2

Seven years later, Richard and his wife welcomed a baby girl named Jane into their family. The boys, especially, were thrilled to have a sister after having grown up with each other for several years. The first child born was a boy, and the age gap between him and the twins was three years. Richard and Ruth spent seven years before finally having a daughter due to the time and energy the twins required while growing up. Their ideal family had initially included three children - two boys and a girl. However, their second pregnancy resulted in twin boys, making it three boys instead. They decided to try again for a girl when the twins were six years old, and Ruth successfully gave birth to a daughter when the twins were seven, completing their desired family composition.

As the boys reached the age of five, it became increasingly challenging for the family to distinguish between them. Despite being intelligent, the twins looked almost identical and often resorted to unfair tactics while taking advantage of their indistinguishable appearance. To manage this, the family implemented instant disciplinary measures to ensure fairness.

Clothing exacerbated the situation since the boys wore the same outfits.

The situation was exacerbated by the fact that the boys had identical clothing for everything. In a specific incident, one of the twins applied excessive force to the family's car outside door opening lever, causing it to snap as the locked door resisted. The event unfolded rapidly, with the boy fleeing from his sister, who pursued him with a water spray gun. Only the sister witnessed the incident, standing at the right front corner of the house and observing the entire occurrence.

Reacting swiftly, the sister sprinted back to the rear of the house, where their mother was busy preparing breakfast in the kitchen. Breathlessly, she called out, *"Mum. Mum,"* to alert their mother about the situation. Upon reaching her mother, the message was clear: *"Mum, Christopher has broken the car door handle."*

Recognizing the trouble he was in, the boy immediately grasped the seriousness of the situation. Observing his sister's return and realizing she would report the incident to their mother, he swiftly bolted through the front door and headed to their shared bedroom, where his twin brother was. Fortunately, upon entering the room, he discovered that his twin was wearing nearly identical attire - Nike sneakers, black slacks, and an Arsenal red and white jersey top. Both boys were avid fans of Arsenal football club.

Taking quick action, he removed his Lacoste T-shirt and retrieved his Arsenal jersey, putting it on. He then hopped onto his bed, joining his twin brother who was already lying on his own bed. The twin was eagerly anticipating the televised Arsenal vs. Liverpool game scheduled for that afternoon.

As their mother inspected the broken handle, she exclaimed, *"Jesus, these boys! Jane, where is he and what is he wearing?"*

Jane responded, *"He's wearing a light blue Lacoste T-shirt, black jeans, and black Nike sneakers."*

After hearing Jane's description, their mother entered the house through the front door and climbed the stairs. Along the way, she called for her daughter, and Jane joined her. Taking Jane's hand, Ruth led her to the boys' room. Ruth needed Jane to provide her account of the incident, as Jane had witnessed it first hand. Upon reaching the bedroom door, Ruth positioned Jane in front to lead the way.

However, upon entering the room, her arm froze halfway as she wore a surprised expression. Her brothers were dressed in identical clothes. Their mother glanced at her daughter and then at her two sons, understanding the dilemma her daughter faced.

Addressing the twins, their mother asked, *"Which one of you two broke that handle?"*

The boys exchanged glances, and a moment of silence filled the room. Jane and their mother observed as the boys looked at each other, fully aware that neither of them would admit to the incident. Despite the question, their mother realized she wouldn't receive an acknowledgment from either of them.

"You're doing it again. Well, I suppose you'll tell that to your father," their mother remarked before leaving the room, guiding Jane away by the arm. When he was alone with his brother, the innocent twin inquired,

"How did you break it?"

His brother replied, *"The car is just in bad shape. They should get a new one. Can you believe it? I was just trying to open the door, and it snapped in my hand."*

The innocent twin knew that his brother had already made up his mind and that pursuing the matter or asserting his innocence wouldn't make a difference. He understood that his twin would stick to the story that he hadn't left their bedroom that morning.

Upon learning about these events from his son Richard, their grandfather, Mr. Wright, responded with excitement rather than disappointment at the twins' mischievous behaviour.

"You know what, those boys could even get away with a crime in a court of law," Mr. Wright remarked.

Curious, Richard asked, *"How is that?"*

Mr. Wright explained, *"In cases of uncertainty, a court of law cannot convict two individuals for a crime committed by only one person. The one who committed the crime is likely to go free. Absolute certainty is demanded by the law. Now, can you honestly say that you would be that sure about those two boys, especially if they collaborated to evade the system?"*

Richard found it difficult to believe what his father was suggesting. *"Dad! Did you foresee this when you proposed giving them the same name?"* He asked.

Mr. Wright responded, *"It's like asking me if I knew your wife was carrying twins. That was purely spontaneous."*

The Virtues of Split Personality

Once again, Mr. Wright expressed his satisfaction with his perspective.

"You continue to surprise me. You always manage to find something positive, turning every puzzle and unpleasant situation into something optimistic. It's as if things are falling into place for you," Richard acknowledged.

"Well, the truth is, I have a habit of looking at the other side of the coin. It helps me distinguish it from the rest. Taking things at face value isn't always productive. It's important to take the time to uncover some positive aspects even in difficult situations."

Chapter 3

After a few years, the twins had developed into fine teenage lads and were due for high school, their parents enrolled them at St. Paul High School. Ruth and Richard had noted that the twins were not just extremely clever but also athletic. This influenced their decision to enroll them at St. Paul High School. The school was renowned for its track record of preparing students for professional careers in sports as well as its excellent academic standards. The school was located along the M13 highway about five km from the central town. The location of the school was chosen to keep the students away from the bustle of the main town so that while they were on campus, their only thought would be schoolwork.

One could only see the advertisements on either side of the road when driving five kilometers up north on the M13 highway if they paid much attention. The billboards were roughly a meter and a half off the ground but due to carelessness on the part of the school administration, they were almost hidden by the overgrown shrubs. These signs were placed about 100 meters apart on either side of the 'T' intersection formed by a road that diverged into the forest to the left when travelling north and to the right when travelling south. Except for the road, which they must have supposed led to a farm, most motorists who travelled on the road in either direction and were unaware of the school must have believed the stretches on the left and right, respectively, to be a full forest.

Because the branches of the trees along the road reached right above and created a shaded, nearly night like darkness, it was imperative to drive with lights on when on that road leading to the forest. The road continued into the forest for roughly 500 meters before it curved and le to a resort area. It landed on a slab of concrete that extended to the left. Motorists made the turn and arrived in the visitors' car park. Further on, the road continued. It passed behind some Basketball and Tennis courts before disappearing behind a 19th Century Victorian building. The courts were next to the building's farthest left side.

Three identical structures - blocks had been constructed in a row, fully independent of one another. The concrete slab that ran directly across the front seemed to be the only thing linking them. The grounds were covered in lush green grass and a few sparsely placed trees, and the concrete slab stretched out for about 5 meters in breadth.

Starting from the slab directly in front of the center block, a concrete walkway wound its way through the landscaping before splitting in the middle to go around a water feature that had a fish eagle sculptured in the air above it. The path continued and joined the concrete slab at the car park. A few concrete benches with backrests had been strewn about the ground for anyone who felt like sitting down.

Two areas for field sports were located on the ground's right-end, across from the courts. Even though only football could be played on the first pitch, the first and second fields were not intended for any particular sport. Right across from the line of blocks was the second pitch. Both American football and rugby could be played on the second field. While the third pitch was only appropriate for baseball and it was located farther back behind the blocks than the second pitch.

The Principal and the Deputy's homes were opposite this ground at the left end behind the three blocks. The facilities at the school were only a testament of the diversity in sport at St. Paul High School.

As time passed and the twins grew accustomed to their new school, things remained the same: whenever either of them felt like it, they would cause confusion among their peers. The football - soccer Coach wondered how possible it was for both boys to be good at their academics and athletics. One of them was equally as competent as the other and that their preferred sport was football, and they were both capable of playing in any front-row position. Very strange.

The schools tournament final was only one week away. The school was supposed to compete against Crum berries High School, a past victor. They had unsuccessfully attempted to defeat Crum berries High School numerous times. Their coach thought about cheating because of their lack of success in previous encounters.

The coach devised a simple plan, instead of making the normal three substitutes a football team is allowed to make in a game, he intended to make more. Simple enough, he just had to run it past the twins, enact it and ensure not to get caught.

One day after training, four days before the competitive game against their old-time rivals. The Coach walked into the dressing room, looked around and eventually asked for the Wright brothers.

"Where are the Wright brothers?"

"In the showers room," answered one of the boys who stood next to him.

The shower room was partitioned into cubicles. Each cubicle had a polythene shower curtain hanging over its entrance for privacy. *"Hey Wrights!"* He called out.

"Hello," the boys answered.

"This is your Coach, make your way to my office when you are done."

"Yes sir!" The boys answered at once.

The twins couldn't help but be curious, not knowing why the coach might want to see them. In anticipation they figured it had something to do with the game and their contribution to the team.

As soon as they finished freshening up, they made their way to the coach's office. Tapping gently on the door, they head coach's voice come through, *"Come in."*

With a sly grin on his face, he offered the twins a seat as he shifted in his seat trying to make himself comfortable. Trying to warm up the conversation he exclaimed, *"how are going boys?"*

"Fine sir," one twin answered, and the other twin nodded his head in acknowledgement.

"That's great to hear, but there's another reason I called you here for," he

said.

"I need your assistance and consideration. As you are aware we have a game scheduled for four days from now, and I hope you know that in all our previous meetings, our school has never prevailed against those guys. Simply put, we have only accomplished the bare minimum... only draws."

"That is strange," One of the boys said.

"Yes!" the coach agreed, saying, *"It would be strange. If we don't do our homework, it'll really be sad. To be honest the Crum berries are still that good and have always worked as a team."*

"You mean to suggest that none the former players of this team were capable of winning any of those games?"

The coach shrugged his shoulders, indicating that he wasn't sure.

"But those guys are not a walk in the park, I wonder often how they do it. It difficult to retain such dominance for such a long period of time. These guys always appear to have some extra energy coming from somewhere to beat their opponents the last minutes. God only knows how they do it. Anyway, I want us to do our part," he said.

He paused to look at the twins, then continued.

"Lately, I have been getting some stories about you two. I've heard you have a habit of confusing people about who is who cause you look so alike."

The boys looked at each other adamantly, locking gazes as though to communicate as to how to handle the conversation.

"Can you tell me something about that?" The coach tossed an open question to the boys.

"Like what sir?" One of them asked.

"I've heard you guys impersonate each other and confuse folks. I was wondering whether you'd ever done something like this to me before?" He inquired.

"No, never sir," the boys answered in unison.

Fearing the unknown, they hastily responded with a tone that gave them away. One would assume they feared for their positions in the school team. They were devoted to the squad and would do anything to see it succeed, the coach knew this.

He was keen to hear that, when and if it happened, he would be more than happy.

"Anyway, I find that very interesting and could be useful," he said.

"How would you two like to help me, or us, in some way?" Realizing that he needed to be more inclusive to give them a sense that they had equal responsibility for the plot and the outcome, he asked.

"Like what sir?" One of the twins asked and then looked at the other, he hoped that was the right question to ask.

The Virtues of Split Personality

Just before the coach could say anything, the other twin asked, *"What would you like us to do sir?"* Indicating to his brother he was open to the conversation.

"To be very honest, I have prepared our team for this game in every way possible. Although I think I have a good team of players, you can never be too complacent when it comes to those guys. They are so resilient, it's not over with them until that final whistle. Just thinking about them has been like a nightmare. I have been trying to figure out a way to finally end their dominant streak. Then when you two crossed my mind, it hit me just like falling in love with the prettiest girl in school."

For a moment he took his eyes off the twins and stared outside through the big window on his left side. The twins turned to look in that direction, their eyes falling on a scenery of treetops. The office which was on the second floor had a beautiful view of the trees below. He continued staring out the window, but it was clear that his mind had drifted past what was visible to the naked eye.

When he eventually snapped out of his thoughts, he asked, *"Do you two have girlfriends?"*

"No sir," the boys answered.

"Fear! I have been there, boys. It's nothing really. They also feel the same

as you do about them. Just play your cards right, but of course not just anyone because rejection the first time might just make that fear permanent. Be sure where your possibilities and chances are. Sometimes all you need is to be alert and just rise to the occasion when an opportunity presents itself. Now, let's talk about why we are here. I intend to make four substitutes on this day. Instead of the allowed three," the coach finally revealed.

For a moment the room went quiet. The twins exchanged intense looks with each other as the coach observed them. They tried to make sense of what he was saying as they returned his gaze, and as if they had telepathically communicated with each other, one of them broke the silence, *"How do you hope to do that?"*

"That is where you two come in. If you two are on board, which, I don't see why not, I'm going to use your assistance. In any case, unless you desire that win less than I do," the coach said. Making it sound like the team's performance on that day would be in their hands.

"Normally you start the game together, this will be an exception".

The twins anxious, if not disappointed, looked with each other. They did not seem to like the idea. It had never happened; they would always start matches together. For a moment the coach remained silent as he could see the disappointment written all over their faces.

"*How it'll happen is as follow: during practice, one of you will pretend to hurt their ankle due to some infraction. So, pay attention to any serious aggression at any of you and seize the chance,*" the coach said.

"*Suppose nothing happens, I mean the infraction?*" One twin asked.

"*Our training will last for two days. It'll happen. If it doesn't happen during our normal training hours, we'll simply increase the period of time until it does particularly on the last day. I suggest you make every effort to keep the ball in your hands as much as you can during these practices so you can keep dribbling your way through. Most likely, one of you will have their rights violated. Watch out for that strong tackle. I will be there as well to show my support. Look at me for that signal in case you are unsure. The decision to remove any of you from the team's starting lineup to play the game that day would be based on that infringement. Whoever will have the sprain on the day of the event should be in their own clothes and be in the crowd. He needs to make sure he has a watch. Right before halftime, he should navigate to the dressing room and secure himself within one of the restroom stalls, following a prior agreement on which specific stall to use. This individual will only unlock the door upon hearing a knock and the other person identifying themselves at halftime. Speed is of the essence. The person in the restroom should swiftly join the group as they convene to discuss the ongoing game and devise strategies for the second half. This implies that the player who participated in the first half should hastily enter the restroom and execute the exchange. The new team member will then emerge from the restroom wearing the team jersey, appearing as though he has recently refreshed himself. I'm growing weary of always settling for second place,"* the coach expressed, bringing his argument to a close.

The coach's final statement aimed to rationalize his proposal and elicit empathy from the players.

"I believe we can accomplish that, especially since it's our sole opportunity to etch our school's name in history and we won't be on the team next year," the boys chimed in. That sealed the deal. The coach and the boys reached a consensus. However, the coach pondered whether their agreement was motivated by their allegiance to him or their personal inclination for such endeavours. Nevertheless, he found solace in achieving a positive outcome, which was his ultimate concern.

"From this point forward, please steer clear of trouble. I cannot afford any mishaps befalling any one of you, as that could jeopardize the entire plan. Remember, this is strictly confidential between us—no one else should be

privy to this information, even beyond that day," he spoke in hushed tones.

For the coach, the three-day wait leading up to the game felt like an entire year.

Chapter 4

St. Paul was chosen as the tournament's preferred host because of its convenient location and first-rate amenities, and the school was always happy to promote the sport by doing so even in times when they had not qualified for it. It did so because sport was seen as another means of achieving human accomplishment and fulfillment, and this perception was ingrained in the school's vision. Even so, the school hosted the competition with pride each time the school qualified, as it did this time.

When the big day arrived, St. Paul's grounds were crowded with agents, business people, students from other schools and many other people from all walks of life who had come to see the game specifically out of love for the game, while also pursuing their various interests. Agents were present to scout and ensure that good players are signed by professional clubs. Due to the constant high spectator turnout, company owners could not pass up the chance to advertise their goods as well. The employees of each company travelled there in their unique uniforms and their caravans towed by vans or minibuses.

The schools' football championship was such a significant event that numerous television stations were constantly on site to capture the action for their viewers.

All the seats throughout the stadium were filled long before the game began. The seating arrangement was roughly a meter away from the advertising boards that various businesses had placed there as part of their sponsorship of the tournament. The ground was covered in boards. Coca-cola sponsored the competition to a 75 percent extent, as evidenced by two tall billboards on either side of the field. The other 25 percent was by the other companies. The money at stake was 1million dollars for the winners and 750 thousand for the other finalist.

The game began at precisely 2pm to raucous cheers and cries from the crowd. The Crum berries struck the upright once in the first half. The shot ricocheted off the back of a defender who chose to dunk it rather than block it, landing just beyond the penalty area. Later, another shot slipped between the legs of the same defender, who didn't bring his legs together until after the ball had already passed. The goalkeeper was slightly obstructed. The ball kept rising from the ground as it rocketed towards the goal and the goalkeeper was fortunate to deny the opponents a goal when it hit his chest. It bounced towards another defender who managed to clear it for a throw in.

St. Paul tried tirelessly to attack but failed to create any chances in the first half and it looked like they were destined to come in second place once again. Before the end of the 1st half, the coach made one substitution, removing a defender. The referee blew the whistle, and the 1st half was concluded. The sound of that whistle came as such a relief for the coach who was fuming with frustration at the boys' failure to execute a proper attacking game.

As soon as they got to the dressing room, he could not hold himself any longer, he immediately burst out,

"You know what your problem is? You lack vision! Your passes are so terrible, they are getting the ball from you like taking candy from a baby. All that possession you have given away is because of your carelessness and not because they are better than you! You are just clumsy with the ball."

He paused to breathe, then continued *"listen please, midfielders I need you to stop panicking. Play a calm game, when you have the ball look around for your teammates who are clear without making hasty passes. Passing the ball into their penalty area when your strikers have no chance is simply wasting our possession. Play around with the ball by passing it even to your defenders so as to get them out of their penalty area. You have to be sharp, when you notice an opening in front, release the ball forward, just be sure to execute your passes with precision if you want to make an impact."*

As the team was leaving the dressing room for the second half, the Coach held back the twin until all the other team-mates were far ahead. He asked him to take off his top and sniffed his armpits, fresh. The boys had kept their promise. That was the coach's well thought idea of affirming the agreement and the secret he had kept from the boys on how he would know if they had not carried out his plan.

He went on to make two additional defense substitutes, it meant he had made four substitutions. Before the 85th minute, neither team scored.

Instead of kicking the ball to the usual distance and as is customary on the other half of the field, the goalkeeper threw the ball to the defender on the right wing. The player then sent it diagonally across to his teammate who was on the other half. The player easily brought it down, took a quick glance and then tactically sent it over as well. The centre had made a long pass to the right wing. With his right foot in mid air, the player wearing jersey number 7 quickly caught it, dragged it down and stepped on it.

Running at full speed, his opponent attempted to hook the ball away by sliding when he was about a meter away, but instead he went past him till he was outside the pitch. Three strides later, the player in jersey number 7 after leaping with the ball was in the penalty area.

Any contact or obstruction that would bring him down could result into a penalty, especially if the player were a cheat. If the referee was one of those overly enthusiastic officials who made hasty rulings simply because an attacking player in the penalty area opted to fake a fall or actually slipped and fell, a penalty would still be given.

Penalties have occasionally been imposed even to the astonishment of the player who had no intention of making such a claim in the first place. The approaching defender considered. Therefore, instead of committing himself as the winger continued to move closer to him, he kept on backing down.

Decisions made by referees rather than performances have sometimes resulted in victories or defeats. Football associations have regarded and exalted referees to the position of 'small gods. Even when the contrary is true, they make important and critical judgments like awarding unjustified penalties and disallowing legitimate goals. They determine which direction the outcome takes. They are also very quiet if there are any reprimands.

Given the emotional commitment they make to their teams and every game, players and fans deserve far better than that.

Fans and players deserve a lot much better than that, considering the emotional investments in their respective teams and every game that is played. On top of that and to their dismay, one really wonders where the concerns of the bodies that are supposed to promote fair play are placed. It's easy to assume that all they are interested in is the money generated by these encounters. These encounters are undoubtedly blueprints to for financial success for the Investors and associations, but what about the fans? What sentimental value is in undeserved loss?

However, if one has a business mentality and is aware of what goes into managing these clubs, one can almost feel sympathetic for the investors who are obviously ripped off by some of those decisions, and they are never given the opportunity to say anything.

Imagine what chaos the associations would have at their hands, if the clubs share holders chose to air their views as well, other than just coaches. Honestly, club owners' silence on some issues as regards the officiating can only be commended or they fear to be punished if they did, as it seems that, it's the only thing that associations seem to do best. Is fair play realistic at all? If it's just a demand on the players and not on the entire administration of the game. Truly, if the concept was followed even in administrative issues some ridiculous decisions would not have been left to stand given the technology that is attached to the sport of football.

Apparently, questions have been raised concerning attaching modern technology to the game of football when all that this technology brings is nothing but mistrust, lack of faith and deserving ridicule to the governing bodies at least from the side of the fans and the players. Or is it what it's intended to achieve?

These bodies undoubtedly don't care about the supporters or the athletes. A lot of individuals are angered by choices made under the guiding idea that referees are always correct, with the exception of it, the ruling bodies and their demonic subordinates-officials. The game exhibits a lot of demonic traits, which befits their role as the devil's advocate and their sadistic attitude toward their regulating job.

In the name of passion, the devil has subtly taken over the

beautiful game of football while purposefully ignoring the psychological harm that poor management of the game does to other stake holders. How are such unnecessary contrivances allowed in the most watched sport in the world? This is why some players and fans take matters in their own hands because more often than not, associations do not offer any redress to their grievances.

So, who could blame the defense for consistently retreating in such a perilous environment? The defender's main thought was to prevent the winger from making any passes and eventually move him outside the penalty area to a more secure place where he could be challenged.

The winger, wearing jersey number 7, turned to face his teammate across the field while his opponent held his ground in preparation for an overhead pass. However, while the ball was still in the penalty area, the winger moved it further to the right.

His teammate on the opposite side also was running in the direction of the goal post's left side. The wingers strike came just before the ball could leave the field of play. *Only fresh legs could do that.* That defender was thrown off by the fantastic kick, and by the time he threw himself across with all his limbs spread out, it was too late. He misread the striker's intentions, which was made worse by a series of thoughts including causing a penalty. Like his defender, the goalkeeper was thinking along similar lines. To catch the cross, he had moved a few steps inside and away from the goal mouth. But then something unexpected happened and the goalkeeper attempted the impossible in the haste of the moment.

He attempted to extend his reach by diving backwards with stretched out arms and body, but he was too far inside, and the ball passed directly through the goal mouth. The net trembled as the number 11 striker, who had effectively covered his attacking area and was aware of the twin, slid and connected the ball into the goal mouth.

On the field, there were mixed feelings as St Paul's players struggled to decide which player to run to: the player maker or the scorer. The play maker sprinted towards his teammates, who gathered around him. Even if he did not score the goal, he deserved the plaudits, and it was worth it.

Meanwhile, the goal scorer had gone wild. He raced into the hands of the spectators after leaping over the electronic advertising boards and kissed one of the women sitting in the first row on the lips. In the heat of the moment, she kissed him back.

"Young man that's my wife!!" a voice screamed at him amid the frenzy of celebration.

Realizing he had messed up, he let go of her head in disbelief. As he hurried back to his teammates, he briefly turned around and pointed at the man whose wife he had just kissed. He shook his head, unable to comprehend what he had just done. He had no other explanation for his conduct except transitory insanity; therefore, he prayed it finished that way without any consequences. The women gave her spouse a sidelong glance while shrugging to demonstrate her innocence.

The entire bench had likewise lost control, including the coach. The crowd erupted in a deafening roar. St. Paul's team was full of life and fire! The boys had carefully followed his directions. 'There is no room for amateurs or underdogs when the stakes are high,' the coach reflected, recalling the adage. He wholeheartedly concurred with it and expressed admiration for his boys.

There has only ever been competition like that in professional club football. Like the thrill you would get watching Liverpool, Arsenal, or Manchester United score a decisive goal or simply an equalizer when any of these three teams were playing the other. When goals are scored, these clubs and their supporters celebrate even more than you would likely witness if one of them won a cup final against any other team save the other two.

When that long awaited final whistle blew, the state of affairs had remained the same; St. Paul won the game with the single goal. For the first time in their history, they had finally beaten the Crum berries, and it was glorious.

Everyone else in the school was still bragging about that triumph in the days that followed, except for the twins and the coach. Their joy was short-lived. Nearly as soon as they entered the dressing room that day, it vanished. Because they had cheated, the pride was absent.

That was the last time the coach and the guys did something similar since the coach afterwards recognized he didn't take personal satisfaction or pride in the triumph. That was the lads' way of getting around problems, so no one would know what was going on in their heads.

The twin's creation of that goal was quite the spectacle, and he had already won so many hearts, including that of a girl named Catherine. She had made her way through the crowd to get to pass a folded piece of paper to the twin as the team walked back to the dressing room.

The Virtues of Split Personality

The twin turned to face Catherine when she shouted, *"Christopher,"* at the top of her voice. She handed the note and added, *"This is for you."*

The twin felt kind of shocked even though the girl was someone he knew. She was so stunning that she was easily noticed by everyone at school, and as a result, she was well-known to everyone.

She and Christopher were not on speaking terms though. She approaching him with the note as a result caught him off guard. He kept asking himself a lot of questions. What could this be? He thought to himself. "Maybe it's my brother," he speculated.

A number of his teammates witnessed her handing him the piece of paper. He placed it in the top interior pocket of the short. He intended to read it when he was by himself in a calm, private setting. When they entered the dressing room, those who had seen the note surrounded him and requested he read it there and then. Despite his best efforts, he eventually caved in. A few people drew closer to him as he took the paper out of his pocket, trying to read it side by side as they stood head-to-head. His friends were in a frenzy.

While whistling and shouting, one of them snatched it from

his hand and passed it on to the others to read. The note read,

"You were amazing out there on the pitch; call me in the evening, I will be waiting."

After a while the note was given back to him with envy. He put it back in the pocket and went on to fetch his clothes. He walked to his brother's locker for he had not been on the team earlier on.

'That girl, something is not right. It should be my brother. He kept thinking to himself, 'how can she pull such a move on me? My brother was on the team earlier on, maybe she thinks I'm him.'

When he got home that evening, he out rightly asked for his brother and he was told that from the time they had left for the game his brother had not come back yet. He had no choice but to wait for him to come home. Unfortunately, he got anxious as time was running out by the minute.

He had two conflicting feelings. He wanted to be sure about the girl, but then, as much as he felt the urge to verify the whole thing with his brother, something else was telling him that that thought was not such a smart thing to do. In the meantime, the clock kept on ticking and by the minute he became more and more sceptical about asking his brother. Finally, he decided against the thought of confiding his dilemma to his brother because he believed his brother would just cheat him out of the date.

Christopher took consolation in a number of excuses. Convinced that he and his brother talk and talked almost about everything, he could not remember his brother say anything about the Catherine. *'Besides, she gave the note to me,'* he thought. This was yet another excuse.

All kinds of thoughts ran through his mind. The compliments from his teammates about the message on the note gave him the urge to go for it, though doubtful whether the note was really meant for him.

Christopher was mindful of the deceptions that ran between his brother and himself. They had no considerations or reservations for each other, neither the other people or simply say - their victims. As such it seemed impossible for him to get his conscious cleared without having to give an opportunity to his brother to cheat him out. Hence, the desire to check with him died out.

It had not occurred to him that having the same name with his brother was such a bad idea until then.

The Virtues of Split Personality

He was more than happy to make the call when the time reached 6pm, far past the scheduled time for the call, and he did so. Before a voice could be heard, the buzz reached him from the other end three times.

"Hello," a female voice said.

"Hello, my name is Christopher. May I speak with Catherine this evening?"

"Catherine here."

"Oh! After this afternoon's football game, you gave me a note."

"I am aware, Chris."

Only extremely close friends have called him that and no one else had in a long time. That was the first time.

"Why did it take you so long?" Catherine inquired.

He was surprised to hear that question because the time was not specific but evening and he believed he had just placed the call on time, the start of evening.

Nevertheless, he made the decision to apologize, saying, *"I'm sorry, it's just that I was caught up in something and got home just about now."* In his reply, Christopher lied. He was very proud of himself for making up a response so easily, and he questioned how he had done it. He was happy he did because telling the truth would have destroyed his chances.

"Well, I'm happy you phoned; how are things going for you?"

"Ok, how about you?" Christopher answered.

The girl seemed to be in control of the conversation as they spoke further because the twin only countered. However, it was a tactic he had chosen as a preventative step for the course of their conversation and taking into account that he still wasn't sure whether he was doing the right thing or not.

"A friend of mine is having a birthday party by their place tomorrow. I was wondering if you could accompany me or do you have something else lined up already?"

He remembered what their coach had said about opportunities presenting themselves and he thought that was his chance to probe.

"I would love to but..."

"But... What? Your girl friend...."

"No!" Christopher quickly interrupted before she could finish.

"Come on Chris, what then, my boy friend?"
"Yes."
"Aha. What about him?"
"I just do not think he'd like that. Guys do not appreciate to see their beautiful girls hang around with other guys especially at a function of that kind."

Catherine gently giggled before asking,

"What makes you think I have a boy friend?"
"I just don't see how a girl like you can be without one."
"Why is that?"
"Well, you are beautiful, very attractive and cool too. You just make the ideal girl most guys dream about."
"I don't know what to say."

It just clicked to her that that was the reason why boys had not been asking her out.

"They sound like compliments; however, I realize those are my biggest disadvantages. Honestly, and if not mistaken, I'm of the impression you have had your eyes on me. Have you been spying on me?"

"*Not really. Well, I may be guilty to some extent, but you are easy to notice, and I suppose every other guy in school especially my friends regard you the same way as I do.*"

"*Oh, so which boyfriend have you guys given me?*"

"*Frankly speaking, I don't know but I have always assumed you had one for the same reasons I have given you. Cathy, are you saying you have no boyfriend?*"

"*I wish I had,*" she said and took a pause.

"*Now that you know that I'm not attached, are you going with me or not?*" She asked a moment later.

"*What time is the party?*"

"*If that is a yes, be ready by 7 p.m. I will arrange with some friends, and we will come and pick you up.*"

Christopher seemed friendly and cheerful that evening. Even more so, he assisted his mother in the kitchen. Even though his mother was unable to imagine what it was, she had a hunch that the pleasantness would eventually lead to some sort of request or favour in exchange for the helping hand. They both did that when either of them needed something, so she was aware of that. As a result, she was not shocked when the request for permission actually came.

"Mum, I have been invited to attend a birth party tomorrow evening, I hope you do not mind."

"Are you asking me for my permission or not? You don't sound like one who is asking. You are telling me."

"It's just that, I thought you'd not object. Anyway, I wouldn't go if you said no."

"Which friend is this?"

"A friend from school."

"His name?"

"Her name is... Catherine."

"Catherine, since when?"

"It's nothing mum. She could have asked anyone else. All she needs is someone to accompany her, I suppose all her friends have partners."

"So, since when did you become an escort?"

"Mum, she is not paying me."

"So, she likes you?"

"Mum, am I going or not?"

"Stay out of trouble or your father will 'kill' me and you know what that would mean."

He walked to his mother and kissed her on the cheek.

"Yes mum. I would never go out again. I love you so much."

"No, I really doubt it... if it's me you love so much. It must be Catherine. If you have suddenly realized, you love me so much, then this girl must be an angel and a blessing to me because I would certainly love my children to love me that much. Be a gentleman and treat her like a lady if you would like to have more of those escort requests from her."

That evening, he made the decision not to bring it up with his brother when he arrived home. He thought he had gone too far already. In addition, Catherine gave no indication that they had discussed anything at all.

It was Saturday, May 1, 1985, the following day. In the Wrights' house, everything went on as it would any other Saturday. At around midday, Christopher, the other twin, left for a friend's house. He thought back to the agreement he had made with the girls after visiting his pals that afternoon. He then made the decision to visit Rabecca to learn more about the date and who would be taking him out now that they had won the game.

He walked on through the gate at Rabecca's residence and knocked on the door. After knocking a few times, Rabecca came to answer the knock herself, and she was surprised to find that it was Christopher who was knocking.

"What are you doing here?"

"You know! About my date," Christopher responded.

"What about your date?" Rebecca asked.

"I was serious, and I want to know who is taking me out?"

"Christopher, in the first place you are not supposed to be here. It's about 7 p.m. and Catherine is supposed to pick you up just about now for a birthday party."

"What birthday party?"

"Our friend has a birthday party this evening and you are supposed to be Catherine's partner. Well, we all know you guys won the game, so we all agreed Catherine would take you out this Saturday evening, I mean today. She is the only one who has no boyfriend of the girls who were there. So, it worked out right for you because there is this function and the girls all agreed to go there with their boys, so Catherine has you."

"Are you making funny of me? Because this is not funny."

"I realize you are really serious; we were actually worried ourselves, that you were probably joking when you made those offers. Anyway, to be honest with you, Catherine would soon be by your place any time now."

"Rabecca," Christopher managed to say in disbelief,

urging her to be more serious.

"Go home, otherwise she would be disappointed if she doesn't find you there. But how is it that you are not aware? Quite frankly, I thought I had heard her say something about getting in touch with you yesterday?"

He realized it was too late to go out that night once he was on his way home because he still had to get there and get ready. It was only 10 minutes before 7 o'clock. I won't make it, he concluded. He abandoned the plan and made up his mind to make amends to her at school on Monday morning and explore other options. Christopher found solace in the idea that if anything, she was at fault because she didn't communicate.

By 6:40 PM, his brother was prepared, and by the time it was 7 PM, he was waiting for his pickup in the living room.

Ruth was curious and wanted to see the girl her son was going out on a date with. So, she disguisedly sat by her bedroom window. The lace curtain across it made it much easier to look through at just about the appointed time without been spotted. She hoped to see and assess the girl, *besides, it was just right for a parent to do So and know the child's associations in case of some unforeseen eventuality.* Ruth found it necessary and justified her stolen moment to look at her son and his date. She remembered too well, that her son had refused for the two ladies to formally meet, saying it was rather too early for such a gesture considering that it was just the first date.

Deep down in Christopher's heart it was because of his uncertainties about the whole thing and how it had come about and not knowing how far it would go.

Ruth was on the lookout when a car came up by their roadside, and she was struck by the beauty of the girl who got out and walked through the front gate and towards the front door.

She said to herself, "If that is the girl, then I understand and I hope she is as well behaved as her looks."

Catherine wore a black dress that hit just above her knees and black ankle boots with block heels. She had her long, black hair pulled back, trimmed slightly behind her skull, and then let it to hang loosely.

Christopher met her partway as she approached the front entrance. He sported a cream-colored, round-necked sweater layered over a light blue shirt, paired with black trousers and shoes. His appearance seemed quite attractive, albeit somewhat mature for his age. Ruth speculated that it could be attributed to his outfit.

Christopher and Catherine exchanged smiles and acknowledged each other's presence as they strolled towards the vehicle, clasping each other's hands in an affectionate manner, reminiscent of lovers.

Upon the arrival of the other twin at home, the clock read 7:20 P.M. He inquired whether anyone had visited in his absence. His mother's initial response involved questioning his late return, followed by confirming that no visitors had come for him.

In haste, he proceeded to his bedroom, organized his attire, and took a shower. Once dressed, he settled in the living room, harbouring a glimmer of hope that Catherine's delay might explain her absence. He occupied himself by watching TV for a brief period until that hope gradually faded away. Subsequently, he had his meal and, driven by concern, inquired about his brother before retiring for the night. His mother informed him that his brother had attended a birthday celebration with friends—a coincidence that failed to register or provoke suspicion, as his thoughts were consumed by his own romantic rendezvous.

Chapter 5

At the party, Christopher displayed genuine gentlemanly behaviour. He made a conscious effort to conduct himself correctly, focusing his attention on Catherine and consistently remaining by her side. He refrained from glancing at other girls, except for those who approached to greet them, leaving many curious about his identity.

During introductions, Catherine presented Christopher as her close friend from the same school, resulting in warm welcomes and subtle requests for personal contact information. Christopher's presence drew the attention of numerous girls, even those accompanied by their boyfriends. In one instance, Catherine introduced him as her boyfriend to discourage potential romantic interests.

Catherine's intention was clear: she aimed to establish a meaningful relationship with Christopher. She contemplated the possibility of clarifying her intentions if he didn't reciprocate, having been pestered by friends seeking to connect with him. However, their interactions hinted at mutual feelings. At the birthday party, Christopher's protective gesture of embracing

Catherine during a speech garnered surprised but positive reactions.

As the party concluded, Christopher and Catherine requested a ride home, while others chose to continue celebrating elsewhere. Christopher was dropped off first, with Catherine and the two girls in the back seat of a convertible Audi. En route, the convertible cover retracted unexpectedly. Seizing the opportunity, Catherine quickly exited the car, circled around to where Christopher stood near a gate, and passionately kissed him. The intimate moment lasted about 30 seconds before Catherine reluctantly pulled away and rejoined the car.

Despite Christopher's attempt to hold onto her, Catherine departed, leaving Christopher deeply moved by the experience. He retreated to his bedroom, reflecting on the meaningful encounter. The name "Catherine," meaning "pure one," resonated with him as he recalled the power of reading and its influence on love and leadership. Christopher eventually settled into bed, thoughts swirling beneath his pillow.

Chapter 6

On Monday morning, as per their routine, they all headed to school. At the end of the school day, Christopher, one of the twins, set out in search of Catherine. Despite his efforts, he couldn't locate her, but he did spot Jane in the distance, nearly leaving the school premises through the main gate. With a call and a brisk run, he caught up with her. Jane glanced back and paused by the sidewalk upon hearing her name called, observing Christopher running towards her. "Hey Christopher, how's it going?" She initiated the greeting, considering his breathless state.

"Hi Jane, I'm relieved to have finally found you. I need to talk to Catherine, do you know where she is?" Christopher inquired.

"Oh, by the way, she mentioned it to me," Jane replied.

"That's precisely why I want to see her."

"I believe she's taken a liking to you, and that significant kiss worked its magic. She can't stop talking about it. I never imagined you could captivate someone like Catherine."

Christopher found himself at a loss for words, his expression turning vacant. He furrowed his brow and briefly closed his eyes. In that instant, he was engrossed in introspective thoughts. Jane couldn't help but notice his sudden shift from enthusiasm to introspection. Sensing something amiss, she questioned, *"Is something bothering you? Are you upset that she shared it with me?"*

Christopher mustered a forced smile. "No," he assured her, meeting her gaze. *"Honestly, it's fine. Anyway, I'll catch you later."* With those words, Christopher took his leave, leaving Jane somewhat puzzled.

Upon reaching home, Christopher went directly inside. It dawned on him that his brother had not yet returned. This situation had Christopher's involvement written all over it, he deduced. He had made up his mind to address the matter with his brother once he arrived, so he settled in the living room and waited. When his brother eventually entered, Christopher wasted no time in initiating the confrontation.

"Christopher, we need to have a conversation."
"What's this about?"
"Don't think I'm oblivious to your Saturday escapade with Catherine. Seriously, why are you putting me through this? It's absurd."
"What are you implying?"

The Virtues of Split Personality

Patson M. Chifumbe

"We've shared our fair share of pranks and crazy antics, but when it comes to dealing with someone's emotions, I don't find it amusing, and I certainly don't think it's respectable. Your actions could land you in trouble."
"Why the lecture? I've acted responsibly and respectfully towards her."
"So, you're not even going to deny it?"
"Deny what? Quit beating around the bush."
"You knew she was interested in me."
"But she's not your exclusive property, and you never claimed her to be."
"I don't believe I owe you an explanation, especially regarding my personal life. By the way, does that give you the right to impersonate me? Why couldn't you just tell her I wasn't available?"
"Come on, I'm not some wild animal. Why would I impersonate you?"
"Then enlighten me."
"There seems to be a misunderstanding. First and foremost, I know nothing about your situation with Catherine, so, I fail to see how the idea of impersonation even arises. Secondly, my attendance at the party with her was prearranged; it wasn't a spontaneous decision as you're portraying it."
"Well, explain how it unfolded then?"
"I hope you're not attempting the same thing with me. If I recall correctly, Catherine didn't display any signs of recognizing me as

The Virtues of Split Personality

you. So, how can you claim she's exclusively yours?"

"This matter isn't suitable for public disclosure due to its embarrassing nature. However, if you're willing to proceed with that, I'm okay with it since I have several girls who can support my side."

Which girls?"

"Jane and the others - who coincidentally are Catherine's friends."

"But I also have a group of guys willing to support me."

"Which guys?"

"The guys from our school's football team."

"Something seems off. 'Is she deceiving us? Could you explain how it all unfolded?"

The twin capable of answering felt compelled to share the sequence of events. He recounted the entire incident, even going to their room to retrieve the note Catherine had given him after the game as evidence. When his brother finished narrating, Christopher comprehended the situation and became more understanding. He transitioned from standing to sitting on the couch and gazed at his still-standing brother, saying, "I suppose you'd like me to tell my side as well?"

"Absolutely, how should I interpret your accusation?"

The Virtues of Split Personality

Patson M. Chifumbe

"Well, it was on a Friday, the very same Friday of the game. As I headed towards the dressing room, I encountered a group of girls. Here's how the conversation unfolded from both their words and mine: 'Hey girls, are you here for the game?' I inquired.

"Yes," they replied."

"That's great, and wish us luck," I remarked.

"It wouldn't change anything," Catherine, one of the girls, responded, and her friends chimed in with agreement. Approaching them, I added, *"You all are quite different from the fans and press of the English national team."*

"What's the comparison?" one of them inquired.

"They predict victories well before their national team even takes the field," I explained.

"No wonder their team under performs, leading to criticism of players and coaching staff," Catherine contributed.

"Explain that to me," I requested.

"It's psychological. This negative mindset affects their team, which enters the game with overconfidence, only realizing they've lost when the final whistle blows."

"That can't be true!"

"But how do you explain their lack of trophies despite

The Virtues of Split Personality

having exceptional players?"

"So, what are you implying? Your comparison to English fans and press doesn't hold up because they have some of the best players, unlike you guys and us, your so-called fans."

"Tough situation, isn't it?"

"No fans to put pressure on you."

"Come on, give us some credit. We've come this far."

"And that's where the letdown always lies," Catherine declared, confidently pointing her finger in the air as her friends nodded in agreement.

"It was clear I had lost the argument, but I had to come up with something."

"I know you girls have boyfriends, but I'm willing to make a deal with you," I proposed.

"What kind of deal?" the girls asked.

"I must admit, all of you girls are incredibly attractive," I stated.

"At that point, they formed a semi-circle around me, and I positioned myself right in front of them. Captivated by their charm, I playfully nodded my head in appreciation of each one's beauty. I made eye contact with each girl, one after the other, spanning from one end to the other."

"If we emerge victorious in this game," I proposed, *"one of you lovely ladies will have the pleasure of going out with me."*

"What if you lose?" they inquired.

"In that case, I'll be the one taking one of you out," I answered.

"That's quite unfair," they protested, *"it's essentially the same thing."*

"From my perspective, it seems fitting, and well, I'm a free man. I'd feel honoured and would cherish the experience for the rest of my life. So, what do you say?" I asked, looking to them for an answer.

The girls remained silent momentarily, and then Jane assumed a leadership role, saying, *"Alright, Christopher, it appears you're quite eager for this date with one of us. We'll discuss it, but there are no guarantees. Moreover, you should also be prepared to offer something worthwhile in order to deserve the date, regardless of the outcome."*

"Well, I'm not entirely sure what I can offer. A football game sometimes hinges on luck, but I promise to give it my all," I reassured them.

"Girls, what's your opinion?" Jane asked, seeking her friends' final decision.

"Well then, let him go and give it his best, and we'll decide after we've seen

how he performs," one of them suggested, and they all agreed, saying, *"Yes, that's better."*

"Christopher, you've heard their stance," Jane confirmed.

"But that's just as good as my offer because I always give my best in all the games I play."

"Alright, Christopher," Jane said, *"you'll be informed of your date after the game, whether you win or lose. However, our decision will be based on your positive contribution and impact on the game."*

"Can I know my date right now, as it's certain and guaranteed?" I asked.

'After the game!' "They all exclaimed simultaneously, and that's how I left for the dressing room. On Saturday, after the game, I went to see Jane between 6 PM and a few minutes before 7 PM. It was at that moment that Jane wondered why I was there, as Catherine was supposed to pick me up from there as her partner for the birthday party at 7 PM. Glancing at the time, I realized it was too late for me to travel from Jane's place to the party location and still make it in time. Plus, I hadn't obtained permission from my parents. I concluded that the plan wouldn't work out, so, I decided to let it go and intended to apologize to her, hoping we could arrange something else. Today, after classes, I tried to find Catherine but couldn't

locate her. Instead, I ran into Jane and mentioned that I wanted to see Catherine. That's when she started telling me about their outing, the kiss, and how Catherine had become infatuated with me. All her friends, including Catherine herself is aware that it was me. However, I didn't go anywhere, I was right at home, here."

"So, when she handed me that note after the game, she must have mistaken me for you?" inquired the other twin.

"Yes, it would have been different if it weren't for that substitution."

"Well, that makes sense. So, what's the plan now?"

"Now you know, back off."

"I don't think it's that simple. If anything, it's better if I continue, because Catherine and I have taken things further than just a date. She's my girlfriend, and if you must know, I've actually been with her this whole time. That's why I arrived here so late. I don't know how you missed her when you rushed out to find her, because she came to our class to pick me up."

"If I can't have her, you can't have her either. I'd rather see her with someone else than with you."

"What do you mean by that?"

"We both stay away from her."

"Come on, Christopher, that's not fair."

The Virtues of Split Personality

Patson M. Chifumbe

"What do you know about being fair? If you were considerate enough, you wouldn't have approached her like that. How many girls write notes to boys out of the blue? I don't know any. You should have found it odd and considered me, but of course, it was all about you."

"It's just logical for me to continue."

"What logical...? Logical... my foot."

"Well, if I back off, then what? You take over from there? I don't think that's the right thing to do. Catherine has already been with me; there's no way she can be with you. It would be wrong because she knows nothing about all this."

"Of course, there's no way she could know about all of this. That would mean exposing the whole substitution thing. So, as I said, we stay away from her."

"But how do I explain backing off like that? Catherine isn't just beautiful; she's kind and exceptional. She doesn't deserve to be treated this way."

"You have no choice, and that's not my concern. I don't know how you'll manage it but just drop it. This discussion is over."

The Virtues of Split Personality

He stood up and walked towards the stairs, followed by his brother. *"Why are you doing this?"* his brother asked. He stopped midway up the stairs, glanced at his brother, and continued. His brother stood at the bottom of the stairs, watching him until he disappeared at the top, heading towards the bedroom. For a while, he remained there, head down, chin resting on his chest, contemplating what his brother would do if he continued seeing Catherine.

The next morning, the twins didn't exchange any words as they got ready for school. Normally, they'd walk together, but that day, each walked alone to their respective pickup points. In the afternoon, the upset twin left his class during the last study hour. His thoughts were too consuming, making it impossible to focus on his studies. He spent that hour seated in the same spot where he had made the deal with the girls that Friday afternoon before heading to the dressing room for the match.

He was still there when classes ended. Students started streaming out of the school building. Among the first group to leave was Catherine. As she walked with her friends, she noticed Christopher sitting at the spot that held significance for her too. She assumed that he probably felt the same way about it, which was why he was there. She slowed down and eventually came to a stop, gazing in Christopher's direction.

Her friends slightly slowed down as well but continued on with smiles when they realized what had captured Catherine's attention. Christopher was seated on the lawn near the football grounds, facing the pitch with his back to the path leading to the car park. This was the path Catherine, and her friends were walking on. She decided to change her course and join him. As she got closer, her steps became stealthy and measured, so as not to startle him. Meanwhile, Christopher was lost in his thoughts.

"Jane," he guessed aloud as he felt hands over his eyes.
"No," Catherine responded, stepping to the side.

She removed her hands from his eyes and wrapped her arms around his neck, lowering herself onto his lap and kissing him on the lips. Fully aware of her presence, he eagerly kissed her back, his passion reflecting the feeling of long-awaited connection. After several intense seconds of kissing, Catherine pulled back abruptly, her gaze fixed behind Christopher.

"Your brother," she said softly.

Christopher turned his head and looked behind him, only to find his brother standing there. Embarrassed, Catherine quickly stood up, taking a few steps backwards. Christopher shifted from sitting to all fours, then onto his knees with his butt on his heels and his hands off the ground, looking up at his brother. Amid rising, a punch struck the side of his jaw, causing him to collapse to the ground. The blow was so powerful that he struggled to regain his footing, his first attempt ending with him wobbling back down. He felt dazed.

After a moment, he propelled himself forward with both legs and fiercely slammed into his brother's midsection using his right shoulder. The impact caused his brother to stumble backward, throwing him off balance. Instinctively, his brother locked his left arm around Christopher's neck. The force of the collision caused them to stagger backwards, his brother gripping Christopher's belt with his right hand in an attempt to stabilize. Christopher, in turn, clamped his arms around his brother's knees, making it difficult for his brother to maintain balance. This led to a fall, with his brother's left arm still constricting Christopher's neck.

During the struggle, Christopher's anger intensified as he thought about his brother impersonating him and robbing him of the chance to date Catherine just two days prior. His intention was to lift his brother, slam him to the ground, and then pin him down to deliver a lesson. However, his brother's strong grip on his neck prevented that plan from succeeding. They wrestled, rolled, changed positions, and the fight escalated.

Amidst the struggle, Catherine screamed, pleading for them to stop and calling for help. Several fellow students rushed over and managed to separate them. Both twins were panting with rage, glaring at each other in silence. Catherine attempted to understand the situation, asking, *"What's happening? What is this?"*

However, she received no response. Christopher, the twin she had just been kissing, approached her and extended his arm.

"Let's go," he said.

The other twin stepped towards them and brushed Christopher's hand away. *"Don't touch her, you scum,"* he retorted.

Catherine was shocked. *"Is this about me?"* she asked.

The twins exchanged accusatory glances, and their focus eventually settled on Catherine. She took a few steps back, shaking her head in disbelief.

"No," she uttered. "This can't be true. But how? Why?" she questioned, her voice filled with confusion and distress.

It was a critical moment for the twins to clarify their situation and provide an explanation. However, Catherine turned away, tears streaming down her face, overcome by shame and embarrassment. The onlookers who had gathered dispersed, and even after the crowd had gone, the twins remained standing at the same spot, heads lowered.

"Why didn't you defend yourself, why did you attack me like that?" the twin who had been struck asked his brother.

"What difference would it have made? She probably would have been angry with me even if she found out she had given the note to the wrong person," the other twin responded.

"And what about you? Why didn't you explain your side of the story?"
"She would have been furious with me for letting her kiss me like that after having been with you," the other twin replied, offering his valid reason.

In the end, they both realized that not revealing their individual perspectives had been the right choice. Sharing their sides of the story would have exposed the entire substitution scheme. Over the next few days, word spread around the school that the twins were both involved with the same girl.

"If you're dating one of them, just know you're essentially dating both of them," the girls on campus whispered.

The incident marked the end of their involvement with Catherine. Neither of the boys could find a way to rectify the situation with her, and she intentionally avoided crossing paths with either of them. Whenever she did encounter them, a look of disgust crossed her face, discouraging any attempts at explanation from the twins.

As time passed, the relationship between the twins improved. They were often seen together around the school campus, a typical reconciliation between twins, no apologies needed. However, the memory of the incident lingered, as groups of girls would occasionally talk and gesture in their direction, causing them to feel embarrassed. They wished for the ordeal to fade away and be forgotten, as it had been a mistake –
unintentional, contrary to what others believed. They were certain that neither of them would ever pursue a relationship with any girls

at the school again. Thus, they refrained from attempting to befriend any girls, as they feared the girls might still remember the incident and rejection would be an inevitable outcome.

Chapter 7

The twins continued with their lives, deciding to focus on their studies and maintain excellent grades in high school. The school's teachers and even their peers were aware that the twins were destined to excel academically.

Three months prior to the final high school exams, the school principal received a roster of students scheduled to take the exam, along with an accompanying letter. This list was intended to ensure that the school administration had verified its accuracy and that no students were inadvertently omitted. It also served the purpose of confirming the correctness of all details and making any necessary corrections.

Upon reviewing the list, the principal observed that only one entry for Christopher Wright was present, leading to his initial frustration with the perceived inefficiency of the system. However, his perspective swiftly shifted upon reading the accompanying letter, which originated from the examinations board and bore the Director's signature. The letter requested the principal's involvement in conversing with the parents of the Wright boys.

The examinations board had arrived at the conclusion that the boys should not sit for their exams within the same district due to their exceptional circumstances. This decision was influenced by a family member's report asserting that the twins possessed an uncanny ability to deceive others, prompting concerns. The family member explicitly emphasized their desire for each twin to be assessed fairly based on their individual merits, leaving no room for errors.

In light of this revelation, the exam board readily acknowledged the concern and took appropriate measures to address the situation, mindful of avoiding any potential exploitation of their reputation and indistinguishable appearances. The board deemed it prudent to temporarily separate the twins, starting just prior to the exams and extending until the release of the results. This precautionary step aimed to prevent either twin from taking advantage of the other in case one of them did not perform as well academically.

Later that day, when the principal arrived at the Wrights' residence, he found Mr. Wright, the twins' grandfather, also present for a family visit. Richard and Ruth were taken aback by the unexpected enthusiasm displayed by the elderly gentleman upon receiving the message. However, the news of this development and the accompanying request left Ruth and Richard feeling perturbed. The idea of an additional expense of considerable size was distressing to them, as they were already concerned about their financial limitations.

"I'm genuinely impressed by the attentiveness and genuine concern shown by some individuals within the system for the well-being of each of these boys. I wholeheartedly endorse this idea," Mr. Wright expressed his support.

"Dad, I find it deeply unjust for you to back this notion without considering the financial burden it places on us. It won't be you who has to cover the expenses that arise from this entire plan. Who will be responsible for our son in that unfamiliar place? I have no idea who we can rely on in whichever town they are sent to. Moreover, both of these boys are undeniably bright. Their academic records speak for themselves, and you yourself have acknowledged it. So, why entertain the thought of one of them not succeeding?"

He turned his gaze and words toward the principal. *"You assured us that they would both excel, so the idea that one might not succeed shouldn't even be a consideration. Please, Mr. Principal,* communicate with your colleagues. It's simply beyond our means."

"Hold on a moment, allow me to handle this," Mr. Wright intervened.

"They're my grandsons; I'm more than willing to take on the entire financial responsibility. Let him go to Dallas; I have a close friend residing there. In fact, try to arrange for him to board at St. Johns High School," Mr. Wright directed his words towards the principal.

"I won't agree to that. Dad, these are my children, and it's my duty to provide them with an education. I genuinely don't require your assistance."

"Enough with the excuses, Richard. Didn't you just admit that you lack the funds to cover the costs? Let me remind you, I intend to make these two boys my heirs. I've witnessed the world and believe it's time to put my savings to good use. Who knows what people might do with it once I'm no longer here?"

Richard carefully observed his father before shaking his head. Ruth, on the other hand, remained silent, resisting the temptation to interject her feelings. She refrained from engaging in one of those extensive debates with her father-in-law, who typically emerged victorious in his own estimation. The elderly gentleman possessed a knack for challenging every situation and viewpoint. Any opposing perspectives or contributions seemed futile once he had settled on a particular stance.

"Shouldn't we inform Mum about this before your offer becomes final?" Richard inquired.

"What I'm offering is my own money. It only becomes hers due to the fact that she's married to me, and it's not as though I'll be spending it all on some extraneous escapade. My intention is to allocate it toward her grandsons. Besides, she has sufficient resources. When you consider her age, what suggests she has many more years than I do? Frankly, I don't anticipate her longevity after I'm gone. Furthermore, why would she decline such an offer?" Mr. Wright articulated his rationale.

The room fell into a brief silence.

"Mr. Principal, that settles it," Mr. Wright declared.

Expressing gratitude for their understanding, the principal asked the family to discuss the matter with the twins and assured them he would fulfil his role. Ruth escorted him to the door, and he departed.

"Father, how can you show such disregard for Mum in front of a complete stranger?" Ruth felt compelled to defend her mother-in-law.

The Virtues of Split Personality

"You speak as though You don't care or love her at all," she continued. "What is the world coming to? Now my own daughter-in-law fancies herself a marriage counsellor. If I didn't care and love her, she wouldn't be my wife. You young people today have turned marriage into a prison. If it were like this back when I got married, I probably wouldn't have married at all. And please, cease referring my decisions to my wife for approval. Men of our age don't act on whims. Such choices are made after providing for our families, and in fact, this is my family. Before making any other financial decisions, your mother's well-being is the priority, and then I decide as I see fit. I don't need to go and ask her permission, for what reason!?" Mr. Wright responded assertively.

The conversation lapsed into a momentary silence.

"For you, since you still have aspirations for your future and the times have indeed changed; I can comprehend that. Instead of spending money, your challenge is acquiring it. I wouldn't be surprised if Richard ends up in court due to these modern laws. I wish I had mentioned this before that young man left; he could have learned a valuable lesson or two."

"Father, don't forget that you live within these modern laws."

"She wouldn't dare, unless you corrupt her thinking! If necessary, I would be more than willing to provide assistance if she were to ask."

"You know, if women persist in behaving this way, they're

compelling men to lead inauthentic lives – living your life, not their own. Consider this: how would you feel if you suddenly discovered certain things about your husband after years of marriage? I, for one, would feel cheated, deceived, and robbed, as that person would have been a part of my life. Knowing the real me when I know nothing about them. However, you can't blame them entirely, as they might have been trying to be what you wanted them to be, rather than being themselves. Some marriages eventually break down due to this. The moment the other person starts living their own life, you'd perceive them differently, saying, 'he has changed. He's not the man I married.' The man hasn't changed. He's still the same, but perhaps tired or bored of living your life."

"The laws are just laws, likely created by well-intentioned men. And it's unfortunate for you, as it appears the men involved in crafting these laws understand the essence of marriage, respect, and loving a wife. Many other men have no issue with that. They have children too; what sets you apart?" Ruth asked.

"Children have nothing to do with these exploitative laws. Frankly, those men involved in the lawmaking process are probably gay or relying on their wives' intellect. How can a normal person legislate a law that evicts a husband, even himself, from his own home just because his wife disapproves of his actions or due to some disagreement. And it never happens the other way around. I can't speak for our gay friends. Worse still, she brings in another man right after kicking him out, and the husband is left helpless, succumbing to depression."

"Anyway, you'll have to accept it. These laws are necessary, and I feel safe as a mother. I'm grateful my Richard isn't unpredictable and isn't like you. His Mother must have strong genes."
"How can he be like his father when his father isn't a coward? From what I see, the wife is a modern, independent, and beautiful woman, and the boy must be terrified. At his age, he can't fathom living with his parents, for I don't see any other way if he becomes his own person. The issue nowadays is that an analytical, fair, and truthful viewpoint on women's matters is deemed evil, primitive, and unpopular among women."
"Father, do you really think your perspective is a universal standard?"
"You know, wisdom comes with age, and in my case, it's a combination of both age and divine insight. I believe I should take my leave now. I'd appreciate a warmer welcome next time I visit. Would you kindly see me out, Richard? Find some time to visit me tomorrow at home to discuss the logistics for the boys."

Mr. Wright then approached Ruth, kissed her on the cheek, and made his way out, leaving Ruth in a state of disbelief over his views on women and the law.

"Tomorrow is Saturday; we work half a day, so expect me around noon on my way back from work," Richard's voice came through.

Earlier during the conversation, Richard had excused himself and headed to the kitchen, staying there while his father and wife continued their discussion. He hadn't even stepped back into the living room to bid farewell to his father.

The following day, as promised, Richard visited his father. His mother was in the living room when the doorbell rang. She *smiled and opened the door, welcoming him inside.*

"Come on in, son. I've been expecting you, and it's wonderful to see you. How's work?"
"It's going well, Mum."
"You must be hungry. There's enough food for two on the table, and your father is in the library. He's been waiting so. you can have the meal together."
"Thank you, Mum. Can I go see him?"

"Of course, go right ahead. How's Ruth and the children, by the way?"

"They're all fine. Ruth knew I'd stop by after work and sends her regards."

Richard knocked on his father's library door and entered. Mr. Wright looked up from his newspaper, stood up, and greeted his son with a handshake. *"Richard, I'm glad you're here. How's the family today?"*

"I woke up a bit early. The kids were still asleep, but I'm sure they're all doing well. And Ruth is fine. She sends her greetings."

"Thank you very much. I imagine you might be hungry too. Why don't we eat first? Your mother prepared enough for two, as I told her you'd be here around midday, just as you said."

They left the library, with Richard leading the way to the dining area.

"The food should still be warm enough. It hasn't been out for too long, but let me know if it's gone cold, and I'll warm it up for you," Mrs. Wright offered.

"Thank you," Richard replied.

During the meal, they mostly ate in silence, with Mr. Wright asking his son only one question about work. Richard remained quiet after answering, apprehensive that bringing up any topic might lead to another of their prolonged, opinionated discussions. Meanwhile, Mr. Wright had a specific topic on his mind that he wanted to avoid accidentally delving into, so he ate his meal in silence too.

"Your silence is quite conspicuous. Is everything alright?" Mrs. Wright inquired.
"I suppose we were both quite hungry," Mr. Wright replied.
"And the food is exceptionally delicious," Richard added.
"Thank you, Richard," expressed Mr. Wright.
"Well, your mother certainly has a remarkable talent in the culinary arts. Her cooking is so exceptional that I find no need to dine out and indulge in heavily spiced dishes, which often reflect poorly prepared and unappetizing meals," Mr. Wright stated, emphasizing his opinion on the use of excessive spices.

Richard responded with a smile, suppressing a chuckle and instead shaking his head in amusement. Once their meal was concluded, Richard's mother entered the dining room to fulfil her customary duty of clearing the table. Richard, however, insisted that she take a seat while he took care of it himself. Mr. Wright, having praised the meal to his wife, headed directly to the library with a glass of juice in hand. The juice was intended to moisten his throat, as he knew that the forthcoming conversation was of great importance. He braced himself for a potentially unpleasant exchange with his son.

Seated at the library table, Mr. Wright awaited Richard's arrival as he entered the room, aware that the forthcoming discussion was likely to be challenging.

"I'd like to get straight to the reason for inviting you here. Without taking up too much of your time, I have two matters to address. First, it pertains to those two young men. Ever since you informed me about the incident involving that girl, I've found myself assuming a significant portion of responsibility and accountability for their current situation. I've been contemplating this matter, and I'm relieved to say my prayers have been answered."

"Dad, you're making it sound like you had a hand in what happened."

"I felt compelled to intervene. Can't you see the situation your sons are in? They're unable to pursue romantic

relationships." Richard raised a curious eyebrow.

"So? Why is that a concern? Why are you thinking that way? What truly matters right now is their education. These boys are still young, and you're suggesting they should engage in casual relationships with girls. Father, there are health risks out there, and they could end up fathering children with young women."

"Richard, you're my son. Don't tell me that your mother and I didn't raise you well, because I take pride in your accomplishments. Look at you, married with four wonderful children. You had the chance to interact with girls, make choices, and eventually marry. I'm not implying the boys should be promiscuous, as that's unhealthy and has consequences. As we should provide them with sex education, just like we did with you. However, I haven't seen the need to do that with them lately. It's been a year since the incident, and I never see them with girls or hear them talking about girls. It worries me that they're convinced no girl in this town would want them due to fear of a similar incident. I became concerned, and that's when I came up with an idea."

"Which idea?"

"The idea to separate the boys."

"Did you have any involvement in that?"

"I'm informing you that if we don't take action, it wouldn't be surprising if we soon had family members involved in criminal activities like rape, or young men with unhealthy obsessions for paying for sexual services in brothels, given their strong attraction to the opposite sex. I acted in their well-being and the family in mind. What are your thoughts on this?"

"I'm at a loss for words, but I believe Ruth shouldn't be made aware of this."

"We'll revisit that later. At the moment, I want to inform you about how that situation unfolded."

"I suppose I hadn't really thought deeply about it, and I assume you've already reached a final decision. What is Mum's opinion on this?"

"I've already informed her, and she didn't object. That leads me to the second point I want to discuss. I apologize that it falls on me to convey this, as ideally, it should have been someone like your grandfather. However, circumstances being what they are, I want to ensure you're aware. While this has broader implications, it may also relate to your marriage with Ruth. Women embrace life with zest, seeking enjoyment and fulfilment. Your wife is undeniably beautiful, and my earlier compliments upon your marriage still stand. Yet, it's crucial to handle her with care. I've heard her praise your qualities as a good husband, and her affection for you is evident. However, don't let complacency creep in, as monotony can dull her interest. Women thrive on unpredictability, which deepens their bond. Reject the notion that certain gestures are off-limits with your wife. Surprise her, even with the unexpected. Speaking candidly, even though some religious leaders surprise me with their actions, don't mimic a 'Holy Father' facade. If you neglect her emotional needs; she might seek stimulation elsewhere. This is why seemingly perfect relationships sometimes unravel. I hope you're not deceiving your wife, as younger generations can be deceitful. Acts like gifts, affection, and portraying the ideal spouse while being unfaithful are misleading. Be authentic, invigorate your marriage. Don't search for fulfilment elsewhere when it resides with you. Nurture your relationship and anticipate mutual reciprocity. In case you're unaware, women desire the same. Prevent future regrets and questions by staying true to yourself."

"I can't help but wonder, Dad, why do you seem critical of women?"

"Richard, understand that my intent is sincere. I'm your father, you're my son. This perspective isn't about mother-daughter dynamics. My words stem from experience. I've witnessed the challenges in my friends' marriages. While you and Ruth are a wonderful couple, I worry about ignorance or complacency straining your bond. Marriage is intricate, and I urge you not to overlook difficulties in your friends' relationships. You never know when you might face similar issues. Condemn dishonesty *and cruelty, even in your wife's presence, as being a saint isn't enough. Equally, don't dismiss serious concerns, as they lead to grave consequences sooner or later."*

Later that day, as Richard made his way back home, he reflected on his father's recent conversation. He acknowledged his father's correctness, although he was taken aback by his ease in sharing those thoughts with his own son. Upon arriving home in the early evening, he summoned his two sons to jointly determine who would undertake the assignment. Once the decision was reached, the chosen son would compile a list of required resources and present it, along with a proposed budget, to his grandfather. The grandfather was prepared to assist in managing the expenses, including providing allowance and covering school fees.

Chapter 8

When exam time arrived, the second twin was not at home and took his exams in Dallas. Ultimately, the arrangement was such that if he succeeded, he would pursue his university program elsewhere rather than from his hometown. The primary objective was to ensure that the twins would not reside in the same town while continuing their education.

Richard and Ruth maintained regular communication with their son, and from his conversations, it became evident that he had developed strong affection for the people and his new place of residence. This provided some solace to them, as they realized that their son was content, even though he missed them as much as they missed him.

Upon the release of the results, both twins had successfully qualified, and their next step was pursuing university programs. Both boys had applied for Business Management courses and were delighted to receive acceptance letters for the same. The affinity for business studies appeared to be a family trait, as their father held a degree in Business Administration, and their grandfather had a background in accounting.

Their visits at home were limited to breaks, as they excelled in their studies, achieving distinctions and merits in their respective courses. By their second year, an external company reached out to the twin who was studying away from home, facilitated through the university administration. They offered him sponsorship, contingent on his commitment to work for the company upon graduation.

Upon hearing the news, their parents felt immense joy, yet they were cautious not to display it overtly. They were mindful of the other twin's feelings and informed him of the opportunity. The second twin commented that his brother was fortunate and speculated that if he had also been away, he might have secured a scholarship like his brother. His mother reassured him, asserting that he shouldn't entertain such thoughts because he was staying put. She shared that she could endure the separation because seeing him was akin to seeing his brother, and she regularly checked on the other twin to ensure his well-being.

Following his graduation, the sponsored twin enjoyed just a month of relaxation and family time before he embarked on his new job. With a track record of consistently high grades throughout his course, his results were not a concern. The terms of his agreement stipulated that he would begin working immediately after completing his program. Both twins achieved impressive results upon finishing their programs, earning distinctions.

Meanwhile, the other twin received interview invitations shortly after their results were released, even though he didn't recall applying for this specific opportunity. During the panel interview on the second day, he was the last to be interviewed and was subsequently called back into the room. He was presented with a contract form and an attached document outlining the job's terms of service. He was given a day or two to review it and was assured that the position would be his if he accepted. The others were informed they would receive a response from the bank within a week or two.

After a week passed, one of the five required trainee manager positions at the bank was filled. The twin who was offered the position was elated and found the job's terms and conditions even more appealing than his brother's. Unlike his brother, he wasn't obligated to stay with the bank, providing him with negotiation leverage for his terms of service. This flexibility allowed him to consider other opportunities if the bank couldn't meet his requirements or if better prospects arose elsewhere.

The Virtues of Split Personality

In Dallas, the other twin's situation had worked out remarkably well, and he was also thriving. His company had secured a two-bedroom apartment in a prestigious neighbourhood for him. Along with that, he received a loan to furnish his apartment and purchase a car. His childhood friends and schoolmates would have been envious seeing him drive the sleek blue-black convertible two-door Audi.

Coincidentally, he had been on the job for two months when his twin brother started working at the bank. He held deep admiration for his brother's job acquisition story and was even more impressed by the job's favourable terms, especially the flexibility to explore better opportunities. Despite having another four years before he could negotiate for his own demands or consider other job options, he found contentment in his current situation.

Throughout their university years, both brothers had dedicated themselves to their studies without any formal agreement. The thought of romantic relationships didn't factor into their pursuits, possibly due to lingering effects of a past ordeal involving Catherine. Additionally, the demanding nature of their coursework left them with little time for such endeavours. Their

She wasn't accustomed to male companionship, especially with strangers. Don Senior took in her appearance in a single glance as he shifted gears. Standing at around one and a half meters tall, she possessed tanned skin, long dark hair, and a beauty reminiscent of South American women, perhaps attributed to their reverence for the Virgin Mary or cultural practices.

Occasionally, her face lit up, breaking into a wide smile. During those moments, it was evident to Mr. Swagger that her troubles were momentarily pushed aside or diminishing. Her slightly prominent eyebrows contributed perfectly to her facial charm.

During their journey, she confided in him, explaining the reasons behind her aimless quest to escape home. This shared connection led them to spend a night together at a layby along the way.

Mr. Swagger's worldview was deeply rooted in scientific theories of evolution, and he kept himself informed about the latest scientific advancements through science journals. His friend Mr. Stevenson, who headed the Scientific Research Institute of Amazon, ensured he received each new issue. Ironically, the friends had not recently discussed matters of spirituality versus science. Little did Mr. Swagger know, Mr. Stevenson had begun to believe in a Supreme Being due to science's limitations in explaining the intricately designed universe.

Lacking religious beliefs, Don Swagger readily embraced temptations, including succumbing to the devil's influence, resulting in his involvement with the young lady. At the time, the devil was 46 years old.

The memory of that encounter remained vivid in his mind. He recalled disregarding his own rule of not giving rides to women and feeling guilty on that fateful day. Though she was 19 and inexperienced, Don Swagger had treated her with respect. For her, the experience evoked mixed emotions, yet she seemed to appreciate it due to her search for stability. Discovering her innocence, Don regretted his actions and promised to treat her respectfully from that point onward. Similar to his late wife Monique, whom he had married with ceremonial agreement, Tania was a virgin – a precious aspect he had preserved.

His introspective thoughts were abruptly interrupted by his rarely present 21-year-old son entering the living room and hurrying to his bedroom. Within moments, the son left the house, the sound of a revving engine fading into the distance along with the scent of burning rubber. Mr. Swagger couldn't help but think his son was acting foolishly. The 19-year-old was named after a motor racing driver whose remarkable skills were acknowledged only after his death in a crash. This reminded Mr. Swagger of a recent incident where a young man had collided with his trailer, the memory of the crushed blue-black convertible Audi haunting him.

Mr. Swagger expressed concern about the younger generation, noting that money seems to excite them while also making them less cautious, as evidenced by incidents involving individuals like Manx and the young man who tragically lost his life due to recklessness on the road. However, he later reconsidered his initial judgment about Christopher, recognizing his potential organization and responsibility based on the state of his car and clothing. Eventually, he recalled the young man's name – Christopher Wright – which he had learned at the police station when giving his report.

Horror was evident on his bearded face as he vividly recalled the gruesome accident. The car, except for its rear portion,

The Virtues of Split Personality

was unrecognizable, much like its owner. Christopher's body had been tragically trapped and crushed between his convertible car and the metal components at the rear of Mr. Swagger's trailer. The positioning of his neck had resulted in part of his face being spared from the impact, though the upper body was disfigured between the car and trailer.

The memory of the chaotic aftermath lingered, with various car horns blaring in confusion, creating a cacophony of sound as people tried to comprehend the situation. Some individuals rushed to the scene while others watched in horror from a distance, their expressions etched in Mr. Swagger's memory.

His thoughts shifted to his own son, Don Manx, whom he nicknamed 'the gold tooth.' Despite any shortcomings, Mr. Swagger acknowledged the profound pain that comes with losing a child and mused about his son's behaviour, reflecting, *"That boy is a red-lipped - lip licking fool,"* as he privately contemplated his son's actions and decisions.

Mr. Swagger's throat raced to quench its thirst as he downed a glass of water, leaving the container empty. Beads of sweat collected on his forehead, forming small spheres akin to marbles. The room felt hot, partly due to his own heavy breathing and the general warm temperature. The absence of the family fan, which had recently stopped working after years of service, contributed to the stifling atmosphere in the room.

His 'True American' T-shirt bore stains and clung to his chest and underarms due to dampness. As his younger son and daughter burst into the room, insisting on watching the Groovy Gullies, Mr. Swagger welcomed the opportunity to escape the stifling environment. Stepping outside, he briefly paused at the doorway, recalling his wife's message that the latest issue of his science magazines had been delivered by the postman and was stored on the rack along with others. He retraced his steps to retrieve it from the living room, easily locating the sealed magazine on top of the stack

Settling onto the veranda's swing bench, Mr. Swagger contemplated his hope that his younger son would grow up to be unlike his older son, Manx. He held a negative view of Manx, perceiving him as foolish and a societal nuisance. To keep Manx out of trouble and occupied, he had resorted to converting the family car into a cab, providing his son with a job that offered some semblance of security. Other employers would fire Manx within a day of hiring him due to his behaviour. Mr. Swagger wondered what had gone wrong with his eldest son and pondered whether his absence during Manx's teenage years, caused by his wife's death and work commitments, played a role in their strained relationship.

Mr. Swagger struggled to come to terms with the disappointing path his son had taken. Manx had become everything a father wouldn't want for their child – a troublemaker who had achieved very little aside from his gold canine tooth.

Despite fathering three children with different women and considering it an accomplishment, Mr. Swagger found this notion inadequate and reflective of his son's poor decisions. Manx's issues had a tendency to spill over onto his father, a situation that Mr. Stevenson, his long-time friend, had often helped him navigate. Thankfully, his son Carter, a successful lawyer, had managed to save Manx from multiple jail sentences for various alleged criminal offenses over the past year. Mr. Swagger was indebted to Carter for his efforts in easing the severity of these situations, although Manx's taxi earnings primarily went towards child maintenance for his illegitimate children.

The Virtues of Split Personality

Reports suggested that Manx had fallen into drug abuse and mistreatment of women, bordering on harassment. Mr. Swagger feared that his son's actions could lead to jail time, a situation he felt helpless to prevent. Despite his concerns, he had reluctantly come to terms with the idea that he might have to accept this outcome and carry the weight of failure, especially in the eyes of his late wife. It seemed as though his son's way of life had predestined him for such a path.

Chapter 13

Penelope, an attractive young woman, remained unattached despite her appeal. Surprisingly, she consistently declined proposals from both men and women, though she had a mix of male and female friends. Her male friends harboured hope and treated her kindly, even though she turned down their advances. Her friends, including those in relationships, felt envious of the attention she received from guys. Penelope, being the youngest and only girl among five siblings, enjoyed favoured treatment from her father. Her father's influence often led her to believe she was right, even in situations unrelated to her. While her brothers initially confronted their father about this, they later realized he did so to boost her confidence within their male-dominated family. Her brothers also protected her closely, and any potential suitors needed their approval to be around her.

After graduating, Penelope secured a trainee-marketing position, hopeful that a change in surroundings would facilitate her healing process. Her plan succeeded, and soon she had a place of her own, marking a turning point as her reliance shifted from family to friends and herself.

Two weeks after an accident, Penelope and her friends, after their usual evenings at Hilltop Café, decided to visit a nightclub with their boyfriends. Seated together, they ordered drinks at a single table. Notably, Penelope's exceptional beauty attracted the attention of a few men who couldn't resist requesting a dance. Observing her relative solitude amidst the affectionate couples, these men approached to ask for permission to dance with her.

"I know you're tired, but please do me the honour, may I have a dance too?" came yet another request, signalling another opportunity.

Laughter filled the table, excluding Penelope, as the third dance request was made. Penelope extended her hand to the man standing by her side, declining the offer with a shake of her head before getting up and heading to the dance floor.

After the dance, Penelope made her way to the ladies' room, sensing the gaze of a man she had passed in the hallway. Even inside the restroom, she felt his eyes on her until she entered. While she initially dismissed him as one of those who had had enough, she found him intriguing due to his good looks and apparent sobriety. She questioned the unusual presence of a man in the women's passageway.

Upon returning to the passage, Penelope noticed the man still there, wearing the same intense look. Wondering if he might be a staff member, she was drawn to his compelling appearance. Suppressing her attraction, she walked past him once more on her way back to her friends. She pondered whether the effect of the few beers she had consumed was affecting her judgment, given her unexpected interest in him.

"You guys are not going to give me away to every guy that comes to ask for a dance from me, I have had it. Look at me, I'm a mess I'm perspiring, and I might soon smell like a pig if it continues,"
Penelope expressed to her friends upon returning to the table.

"Look here, Penelope, you have no one to blame for your looks but God, and besides, that is what you get, 'free for all,' for as long as you keep turning every man down. You better get yourself a man," Edith remarked.

This time, the others didn't laugh but instead focused their attention on Penelope, acknowledging Edith's opinion.

"Jesus! Edith, don't start now," Penelope responded,

The Virtues of Split Personality

As caught sight of the guy who had been standing in the passage.

He had moved into the main room and positioned himself at the end of the bar counter, his gaze fixed on Penelope once more, their eyes locking this time. Edith noticed Penelope's gaze and made a teasing comment, hinting at a potential connection.

As they decided it was time to leave, Penelope felt the urge to steal a quick glance in his direction without her companions noticing, particularly Edith. She observed the man still staring at her, maintaining the same posture as when she first spotted him by the counter. This unnerved Penelope, leaving her wondering if his gaze had ever left her since their initial encounter.

The man was seated on a barstool, positioned at the corner where the bar counter met the wall. His back faced halfway towards the wall and halfway towards the bar counter, with his left arm resting on the counter. He had strategically placed himself directly in Penelope's line of sight, ensuring there were no obstructions despite several tables between them.

Troubled by the man's behaviour, Penelope pondered his motives during the drive to her place. She found his actions highly unusual and questioned why he didn't approach her directly if he wanted to make contact. She thought it was strange that he acted in a manner that seemed almost criminal, rather than engaging with her openly.

Lost in her thoughts, Penelope only snapped out of it when they arrived at her place. Her friends waited briefly before driving off, and she entered her flat, locking the door behind her and heading straight to bed.

The next sound Penelope heard was a knock on her front door. Wondering if it was Christine or Edith, she opened the door without hesitation. To her shock, a man forced his way in, swiftly closing the door behind him with his heel. He grabbed her by the neck with his left hand, pushing her against the wall and holding her there as if expecting a reaction. Though the natural response would be to scream for help, Penelope refrained from doing so. When he eventually released her, he began to visually inspect her body while she complied, maintaining her position against the wall. She believed this was the safest course of action, not wanting to provoke her attacker during such a vulnerable moment. With his right hand, the man began to touch her face, tracing a path from her forehead down to her chin.

The Virtues of Split Personality

He threaded his fingers through her hair, gently pulling it away from her scalp, allowing it to cascade down and then fall back against her body. He repeated this motion with his right hand, all the while moving closer to her. Leaning in, he breathed against her face, his body slightly tilted as he supported himself against the wall with both hands. Their eyes locked, and Penelope noticed his pupils dilate. Suddenly, he lightly kissed her lips, igniting a desire within her to reciprocate.

His right hand trailed down, caressing her left shoulder, then gliding to her waist and eventually her left hip. He lifted her off the ground, and with her in his arms, he carried her away from the entrance, bypassing other rooms until they reached her bedroom. Throughout the encounter, Penelope neither resisted nor seemed offended by his actions, instead cooperating and appearing to engage willingly, possibly to lull her captor into complacency while she plotted her escape.

His actions exuded a sense of familiarity and confidence, indicating he was not a complete stranger. In the bedroom, he placed her down, took a few steps back, and used his foot to shut the door. He maintained unwavering eye contact with her from the moment he entered.

The Virtues of Split Personality

After closing the bedroom door, he advanced a few steps and seated himself at the corner of the bed. Penelope remained stationary, her movements tracking his with a robotic precision. He motioned for her to approach, and she obeyed, stopping directly in front of him. Holding her waist with both hands, he pulled her into the space between his legs. His touch moved from her waist to her chest, his fingers brushing against her breasts. He then paused, mirroring the actions of a skilled doctor with a stethoscope, and listened to her rapidly beating heart. Continuing his exploration, his hand descended, his forefinger grazing her skin as it traced a path downward. Despite her efforts to appear unaffected, her body betrayed her, responding to the sensation as his finger brushed against her silk nightdress.

For a fleeting moment, Penelope held her breath, but a heavy exhale escaped her, inadvertently encouraging him to continue. His finger traced its path until it came to a halt just below her navel.

As his forefinger ventured past her navel, Penelope's fear intensified. She felt compelled to look down at him, hoping to convey her message through her eyes and request him to stop. It was her first attempt to communicate since his arrival. In response, he drew her closer, her knees touching his thighs, and embraced her tightly, resting his head on her chest beneath her firm breasts. His body heaved against hers, and his breath, audibly released, indicated a sense of relief.

He continued his exploration, his hands traversing the contours of her body, moving from her shoulders down her back, over her buttocks, and onto her curvaceous hips. His touch extended to her thighs, just below her buttocks, and his breath grew more rapid and deep as his hands roved over her thighs. Throughout this intimate encounter, Penelope's grip on his head, neck, and shoulders tightened, reflecting her internal tension and uncertainty.

Looking up at her, the man observed her closed eyes and trembling. Lifting her up, he gently placed her on the bed with her facing the window. He positioned himself behind her, his face nestled against the back of her neck. His left arm slid under her chest, emerging on the other side to firmly and gently grope her right breast. His right arm curved over her waist, covering her navel area. He proceeded to explore her body, tracing its curves and folds. They lay together, and he refrained from attempting to go inside her nightdress.

The Virtues of Split Personality

Eventually, Penelope abruptly woke up, turning to check the other side of the bed. She left the bedroom and searched through the kitchen and other rooms. Her examination extended to opening the front door partway to peek outside. Returning to her bedroom, she leaned against the wall and contemplated the events of the previous evening. She recalled her activities up until entering her bedroom to sleep. However, the dream remained vivid and perplexing, leaving her with questions about its authenticity.

On Saturday morning, Christine visited Penelope on her way to grocery shopping, concerned about her tired appearance the night before. Despite Penelope's attempt to hide her relief, she agreed to join Christine at the mall for company. Throughout their shopping trip, Penelope struggled to engage in meaningful conversation, a departure from her typically easygoing and talkative nature.

Christine, noticing Penelope's unusual behaviour, questioned her well-being. Though initially defensive, Penelope eventually admitted to feeling fatigued from the dancing. However, the weight of her unspoken thoughts weighed heavily on her, leading her to provide a dishonest response to Christine's probing.

Patson M. Chifumbe

Uncharacteristically, Penelope grappled with her emotions in silence, refraining from sharing her concerns with her friends. Her inability to maintain a natural conversation, particularly with someone as close as Christine, was a stark departure from her usual behaviour. Penelope was known for being approachable and friendly with men, even when turning them down. Her polite rejections often led to lasting friendships, with hopeful suitors cherishing the chance for a deeper connection in the future.

Penelope's captivating beauty was a sight to behold, radiating a perfection that seemed divinely crafted. Her presence had the power to turn heads and could even bring relationships to a halt without her being aware of it. Her allure was so compelling that even married men would sneak glances in her direction, potentially sparking envy or amusement from their spouses. She possessed a dangerous level of beauty that was impossible to ignore.

While walking through the mall, Penelope and Christine caught the attention of two men leaning against a pillar, smoking cigarettes. The guy with the blonde hair in a ponytail signalled his friend's attention towards the two ladies, making a comment about Penelope's appeal. They shared a laugh at the idea of a woman who

The Virtues of Split Personality

would be so captivating that even a wife might understand a husband's indiscretions, in a moment of desperation.

Penelope glanced back and noticed the men laughing and looking at them, causing them to cease their amusement. The ponytail guy, named John, mentioned that he was open to such opportunities but advised his friend Tony not to make the same mistake, as no woman would tolerate that kind of behaviour.

As they continued shopping, John's newfound confidence waned, and he ultimately abandoned his pursuit of Penelope. Tony offered words of encouragement, suggesting that John shouldn't let his assumptions prevent him from pursuing connections with beautiful women.

After three hours of shopping, Penelope and Christine concluded their excursion. The cab dropped Penelope off at her apartment, while Christine continued on to her own destination.

Chapter 14

Upon returning to her apartment, Penelope hesitated to share her vivid dream with Christine, fearing her friend's amusement and potential mockery. This dream was unlike any she had experienced before – an uncommonly realistic and strange encounter with an unknown man.

The following Saturday night, Penelope retired early, but not before beseeching God to shield her subconscious from similar dreams. Her prayer seemed to be answered, as she woke up feeling refreshed and devoid of any dream recollections. After attending church on Sunday morning, Penelope made phone calls to both Edith and Catherine, her typical routine for a leisurely Sunday.

In the kitchen, Penelope scoured her sparsely stocked fridge for a quick bite, finding only a small cup of yogurt and an orange drink. Familiar with her minimalistic food habits, she thawed a pack of chicken pieces and indulged in her light meal on the couch while watching TV. Her nap unexpectedly extended for three hours, leaving her surprised but rejuvenated upon waking. After washing her face and resuming her CNN viewing, she started cooking when the channel transitioned to reviews.

By 8 PM, Penelope relished her homemade dinner before tidying up the kitchen, leaving everything organized for the next Sunday's culinary adventure.

Entering her well-equipped master bedroom, Penelope made a brief stop in the bathroom for around 15 minutes. When she emerged, her hair cascaded loosely, and she exuded a fresh and captivating beauty. Changing into a red nightdress resembling the design of her sky blue one, she settled into her bed, knowing that sleep wouldn't come immediately due to her afternoon nap. To pass the time, she picked up her ongoing read, "Witchcraft-instant love" by Babyn Kamba, but eventually succumbed to drowsiness after two chapters.

In a frog-like posture, Penelope gazed at her partner, alternately focusing on him and the headboard. Engaged in a passionate act, her thoughts were consumed by the experience. However, her dream abruptly ended, and she awoke, her emotions heavy. Curling into a foetal position, Penelope wept, feeling devastated by the interruption.

At work on Monday, Penelope's colleagues noticed her unusual behaviour – distant and preoccupied. She appeared lost in thought, often staring into space and requiring physical touch to regain focus. During lunch, her colleague Wendi suggested that she go home and rest, offering to cover for her with their supervisor. Penelope agreed, appreciating the gesture and left the cafeteria without ordering.

Preferring not to be alone, Penelope decided to head to a bustling place to distract herself from her unsettling dreams. She found herself in a central town park, where a group of men were playing chess. As she approached, their attention was captivated by her elegance and beauty. She joined the game, attracting both admiration and appreciative glances.

The chess game took place on a concrete slab with large plastic pieces, requiring players to lift and move them over the drawn squares. Penelope experienced occasional lustful stares from the men, which she was accustomed to from her regular encounters in crowded spaces.

As she participated in the chess match, Penelope's stunning presence led to laughter and playful interactions. Her ability to command attention was a testament to her charm and beauty, leaving the men captivated by her appearance.

The Virtues of Split Personality

A game of chess can stretch into a lengthy affair, particularly when skilled opponents are engaged. The players become deeply engrossed, losing track of time amidst intense concentration. Competitive tournaments involve a stopwatch to regulate the pace.

Unbeknownst to the guys, they fell victim to an inexplicable psychological effect, a phenomenon best understood by psychologists. Their moves grew increasingly misguided, resulting in quicker match resolutions when Penelope was present. Even though Penelope perceived them as amateur players, her mere presence disrupted their focus, causing games to end prematurely.

Penelope observed six matches, including the initial one she stumbled upon, but she had to depart before the seventh match due to time constraints. She didn't wish to miss meeting her friends at their customary gathering spot after work. While it wasn't customary to announce departures, Penelope chose to bid farewell, feeling like an outsider amidst the familiar faces. She wanted to express gratitude for the warm reception she had received, despite the public nature of the setting.

The guys playfully acknowledged her departure, expressing anticipation for her return and teasing her with compliments. One guy, who had earlier received a blown kiss from Penelope, mustered the courage to shout his well-wishes, leading to laughter among his colleagues.

Penelope was glad she had made the right choice by going to the park. The chess game had managed to keep her mind off the dreams and as she walked to meet her friends, she resolved she was going to tell them about the strange dreams that she had been having.

Penelope arrived first, then Edith. It was not long before Christine also joined them. After they got together, just two tables from where they were seated, they noticed this guy. Edith spotted him first and beckoned her friends to check him out. *"Isn't he gorgeous?"* She asked.

The guy was having a cup of coffee, she was able to tell because of a transparent jar of coffee on his table, *"Look at him all by himself, he must be a saint and free for all".*

"Come on, don't be naïve. That doesn't mean anything,

Patson M. Chifumbe

'Don't you always move around with Richard, and so where he is now and what are you doing here?" Christine asked.

"Babe don't forget I have a ring on my finger. I can't see one on his. So, the guy is not engaged neither is he married, that is what I meant, when I said, he is free for all. Penny babe, get him, a good-looking dude like him is what you need," Edith bragged and teased.

"I've got my own share of issues to deal with, so let's skip your wild suggestions," Penelope responded, dismissing Edith's playful urging.

Edith continued to tease her, *"Oh, so you've got enough troubles, huh? Is it all about men? Since when?"*

Christine chimed in, noticing Penelope's recent demeanour, *"Seriously, Penelope, is that why you've been feeling down this past weekend?"*

Confusion rose as Edith sought clarification, asking Christine, "What do you mean by that?"

"Ask her, because she never got around to telling me anything," Christine prompted, eager to hear Penelope's explanation.

The Virtues of Split Personality

Penelope initially remained quiet, but when encouraged to share her experience, she recounted every detail of her dream, beginning with the encounter at the club's restroom entrance.

Edith interjected, teasingly asking, *"So, I was right about you are sneaking off for some rendezvous?"*

Penelope met Edith's question with a meaningful look, resuming her narrative to describe the dream where she opened the door for the mysterious man. She detailed each aspect with precision, ensuring no memory of the dream was left untold. As Penelope concluded the account of her first dream, her friends were left in disbelief. Edith broke the silence with a simple "wow," and Penelope proceeded to share another dream she had just before waking up for work on a recent day. She described how the man had approached her after she exited the bathroom, untying her robe and tracing her body with his forefinger. Their interaction intensified as he lifted her and they engaged in passionate kissing, only for him to vanish abruptly as she prepared to remove her nightdress. The dream's sudden ending left Penelope puzzled and awake.

"Gee," Edith exclaimed, clearly taken aback by Penelope's detailed dreams.

As the conversation delved deeper, Christine posed a direct question, asking if Penelope enjoyed the experience beyond just the dream aspect and if she had feelings for the guy in her dreams. Penelope responded with a hint of a smile, admitting, *"Of course I do, in all the dreams. I wake up painfully frustrated by his disappearance, wishing he had just finished what he started."*

Edith jumped in, her tone light-hearted, *"Christine, don't you ever dream? What did you expect? I've always found dreams to be more enjoyable than the real thing."*

Edith's follow-up questions and her candid statement were intended to dismiss Christine's inquiry and highlight the nature of dreaming.

"One other thing that surprises me in these dreams is that I don't seem to resist him. I actually play along," Penelope added to her narrative.

Edith, in her usual teasing manner, responded,

Patson M. Chifumbe

"Yes, babe, because you are such a tease. You know what? If I were a man, I would also take advantage of you in your dreams. It serves you right for being such a handful. You must have crossed paths with the wrong guy this time. Maybe you should advise all those guys who get tongue-tied and nervous around you to consider this dream option."

Penelope sought clarification, asking, "What do you mean by that?"

Edith playfully continued, "You should be confident in yourself. If you're not interested in men, maybe you should become a nun or start wearing a burqa from head to toe to cover up. You must be aware that many of our eager straight brothers around here can't resist cute ladies like you."

Penelope responded with frustration, "Come on, Edith, I don't need to hear that right now. You're such a witch."

Edith humorously retorted, "I'm not the one having rendezvous with an incubus, but you are. Only God knows how long it's been happening. So who's the witch between us?"

Edith expressed her own feelings, admitting,

"Frankly speaking, I'm jealous of you. If I were in your shoes, I don't know..." leaving her thought

The Virtues of Split Personality

unfinished.

Christine joined the conversation, remarking, *"Are you are implying you would have been involved with all the guys who showed interest in you? Seriously, Edith, you can be quite crude at times."*
Edith clarified, *"Of course not. You know, Richard was the only decent guy who pursued me. What I mean is, unlike Penelope here,"* gesturing towards
Penelope, *"I would have gladly accepted the most handsome suitor to pamper me and treat me like any straight woman deserves."*

As Edith communicated her thoughts, her gaze shifted from Penelope to the guy at the neighbouring table, playfully mentioning Penelope's tendency to turn down suitors. She wondered aloud if Penelope might be keeping something from them or if her sexual orientation was different. She hoped to avoid feeling uncomfortable around Penelope's touch, given her own straight identity.

Overwhelmed by the conversation, Penelope couldn't bear it any longer. She abruptly stood up, bid goodbye to Christine, and left, despite Christine's attempts to persuade her to stay. Her

The Virtues of Split Personality

decision was final, and she departed while her friends remained behind.

Christine confronted Edith about her insensitive comments, urging her to be more considerate and apologizing for her friend's distress. Meanwhile, Penelope found solace in having shared her feelings with her friends, even though Edith had been harsh. As she stood by the corridor, waiting for a taxi, Penelope felt a sense of relief as if a weight had been lifted off her shoulders.

Shortly after arriving home, Penelope's phone began to ring. She rushed inside to answer it, finding Edith on the other end of the line. Edith, despite her pride, took a moment to convince herself that apologizing was the right thing to do.

"In case you're surprised, I couldn't wait. I think I owe you an apology. You know it's just that I love you so much and..." Edith started her apology.

"What?" Penelope interrupted before Edith could finish her sentence.

"I feel that a lady of your age and beauty should have someone to love and love her back. Anyway, I think that's where I have a problem. It's your life. It shouldn't be about what I think and feel, and for that, I'm really sorry," Edith continued.

The Virtues of Split Personality

Edith and Penelope shared a laugh on the phone, and Penelope added, *"Edith, you know you can be a pain in the ass? And you're such a jerk."*

"Yes, please," Edith responded, their laughter continuing.

"And if you still want to know, I'm straight. I have feelings for men, except I'm yet to meet that man," Penelope clarified. Edith chose not to mention the man in your dreams.

"So, am I forgiven?" Edith inquired, seeking a direct answer.

"For what? I guess you were right, except you're so crude in the way you express your views – in a really offensive way. I walked out because that was the only way you were going to stop," Penelope explained.

"So, you weren't offended?" Edith questioned, looking for a clear response.

"By you? Of course not," Penelope reassured.

"But if you were, don't act tough with me. It's important that I know, unless you've changed your mind about how I express my views."

"Whatever. I just got home, and your call rushed me in. Why don't we continue this talk tomorrow? I'm starving," Penelope suggested.

Edith must have agreed, as Penelope soon hung up the phone. She had to cut the conversation short to avoid a lengthy exchange with Edith.

Later that evening, as Penelope entered her bedroom, she found the mysterious man seated on her bed. With a mix of emotions, she questioned him, *"Who are you and what do you want with me?"*

Despite her pleas, the man remained silent. Penelope's voice quivered as she implored him to reveal his name, tears streaming down her cheeks. Frustrated and confused, she continued to ask him questions, desperately seeking answers to her ordeal. Yet, the man offered no response, leaving her with a profound sense of mystery and bewilderment.

The guy had gotten off the bed and stood by the wall, gazing out into the darkness through her bedroom window. He positioned himself just at the end of the partially drawn curtain. Penelope, sitting on her bed, faced him with her legs folded and crossed in front of her. After a series of unanswered questions, Penelope fell silent, taking a moment to pause. She began to sob, her face buried in her hands. Moved by her emotions, the guy approached her, cradling her head with his left hand and holding her left hand with his right. Gently, he guided her to sit at the edge of the bed, her legs hanging down. Standing between her legs, he cupped her head in his hands and pressed it against his stomach. Penelope's hands slowly moved from her lap to his hips, and then her arms encircled his waist. Just as she was finding solace in his comforting embrace, she abruptly woke up. Feeling the dampness of her pillow and tears on her cheeks, Penelope realized that she had been crying both in her dream and in reality. *"God, these dreams,"* she murmured, expressing her frustration.

That morning, Penelope decided to take a day off from work and contacted her supervisor to inform him of her absence. She explained her situation and mentioned the possibility of extending her leave if needed. He agreed and assured her to take the time she needed. Penelope also reached out to her friends, letting them know that she wouldn't be joining them after work due to her ongoing struggles.

When Edith and Christine arrived at Penelope's place later that day, Edith was quick to ask, *"What now, is it still about the dreams?"*

"I'm afraid yes," Penelope responded, her voice carrying a mix of weariness and concern.

The Virtues of Split Personality

"So, did you have another dream?" This time, Christine asked.

"I woke up in tears, apparently, I was crying for this guy in this dream, 'can you believe it?" Penelope responded.

"How strange, he isn't sparing you; he means business. So, what did he do to you this time besides exploring and devouring your body?" Edith asked in her very typical way.

"Nothing," Penelope answered.

"Don't tell us you were crying because he didn't touch you," Edith added.

"Of course not," Penelope answered.

"But what?" Edith asked in a rather frustrated manner.

"Look here Edith, you didn't give me the chance to tell you about it. You just walked through that door fired up with and all I did was answer them. So why don't you sit down, I'll make you some tea, and I'll tell you about it."

There was no argument about that, and Penelope went on to make the tea. Just as she put the tray down, Edith was at it again. "So does this guy in your dreams have a name?" She asked.

"Isn't it fitting?" Penelope remarked, reflecting on her dream. As she poured tea into the mugs, she continued, *"I tried to learn his name, but he remained silent. When I inquired about his origin,*

his silence persisted. His sudden vanishing acts, the timing, and the reason behind them all perplexed me. He was unusually quiet. At that moment, tears welled up, and he approached, offering solace, until I awoke abruptly."

"Did he remain distant while you questioned him?" Christine inquired.

"I was on the bed, and he stood by the bedroom window, gazing outside," Penelope explained.

"Tell me, Penelope, how do you feel about him now?" Christine asked.

"I believe I have an affinity for him," Penelope replied.

"Considering what unfolds in your dreams, I sense this man harbours no ill intentions toward you. It's difficult to articulate, but I think he has affection for you," Christine opined.

"But why this mysterious approach?" Penelope pondered.

"I'm not entirely sure either, but could it be possible that you've unintentionally rebuffed him?" Christine continued her probing.

"Never. I only encountered him at the club, and we exchanged no words," Penelope affirmed.

"What does he look like?" Edith inquired.

"Edith, that's not currently pertinent," Christine interrupted.

"If your interpretation holds true, the only other possibility could be that he's attempting to establish a connection – like you two should cross paths," Christine speculated.

The Virtues of Split Personality

"What do you mean?" Penelope sought clarification.

"Just that. I can't elaborate further," Christine added.

"The fact that he hasn't taken advantage of you or forced himself upon you speaks volumes. It suggests he's a decent person who cares."

"When did you develop psychic abilities? How can you be so sure?" Edith sceptically questioned.

"Psychic abilities? It's simply a matter of logic," Christine responded.

"Jot down some of these details, the ones you recall upon waking from these dreams, just in case you forget. These could serve as clues to locate this man," Christine directed her advice to Penelope.

Edith and Christine departed from Penelope's apartment at 8 PM. As they were leaving, Christine expressed concern for Penelope's well-being and suggested they could accompany her to their place, especially since Penelope had recently been granted one-week leave.

"I'm alright. Changing locations might disrupt the course of events. It's better if I remain here, observing the direction of my dreams and hopefully uncovering clues to move on," Penelope tried to explain her reasoning.

The Virtues of Split Personality

"It was a misunderstanding," Edith remarked.

"What do you mean?" Penelope inquired.

"You," Edith replied. *"How could such a beautiful body house such foolish thoughts? I'm starting to believe that one of those adventurous angels must have swapped something when you were created. Dreams are dreams, where you are doesn't truly matter. Let's go, Christine,"* Edith concluded, shaking her head as she headed toward the front door. The other two exchanged goodbyes.

"I'm amazed how the two of you continue to maintain your friendship despite your constant disagreements," Christine commented as she caught up with Edith.

"You know, sometimes you argue about matters even when you're both correct. It's because both of you tend to think in one direction. No one has control over their dreams. Dreams manifest on their own, but in this case, the environment might play a role too."

That evening, Penelope had another dream. In her dream, the man visited her and took her to his home. They arrived at an apartment complex, walking through a gate and ascending stairs. As they approached a door, the man vanished. Penelope woke up, the memory of the apartment complex vivid in her mind.

The Virtues of Split Personality

The following morning, she went to the town planning office to inquire about the complex. Armed with the road name and the complex name, the town-planning officer quickly located the place on the map. With directions in hand, Penelope set off, though doubts crept in during the drive. She began to wonder if the man could truly be there and questioned what she would say if he was unaware of her existence. As she contemplated, the car pulled up in front of *'Liberty Flats,'* as the gate's metal sign indicated.

Penelope decided to let fate guide her while also being determined to take action. She felt compelled to investigate the address and check on the man. She had no choice but to trust Christine's perspective, the only way to unravel her mystery.

Stepping out of the car, Penelope was struck by the tranquillity of the surroundings. The uniformity of the houses, painted in a hue between light brown and cream, caught her eye. Well-maintained gardens displayed vibrant flowers in red, purple, white, and blue, adding to the picturesque scene. The air felt refreshing, and Penelope marvelled at the perfection of the environment. She surmised that this was a neighbourhood inhabited by the affluent, successful individuals with high-paying jobs.

Approaching the gate and providing her information to the sentry, Penelope entered the complex. The upper flats boasted balconies, while the lower ones featured spacious verandas. Tidy lawns were adorned with clusters of flowers, each two meters in diameter, neatly arranged. Parking sheds flanked the sides of the apartment block, with numbers assigned to each slot. A staircase led to the upper flats, and Penelope ascended, heading directly to the dream's specific flat—number 6.

Determined to see her mission through, Penelope knocked on the door. To her surprise, the door opened, revealing a middle-aged woman. Overwhelmed, Penelope struggled for words. Should she mention her dream or inquire about the woman's husband? In the end, she introduced herself, saying, *"I'm Penelope. Are you Mrs....?"*

"Oh, no, I'm not married, I'm Bridget, and I moved in just two days ago. As you can see, I'm still unpacking and cleaning up the place," Bridget explained.

Penelope hesitated for a moment before continuing, *"I was wondering if you might know..."*

"About the previous tenant's whereabouts?" Bridget finished her sentence.

"Yes, exactly," Penelope replied.

"I'm afraid I don't know. There wasn't any forwarding information left, and I haven't been able to find out. Perhaps you could try contacting the landlord," Bridget suggested.

"Who is the landlord?" Penelope inquired.

"I'm not sure about that, but I can find out easily at my workplace. The flat is rented through the company," Bridget informed her.

"I would greatly appreciate that," Penelope expressed her gratitude.

Bridget offered a solution, "*Why don't you give me a call tomorrow around 8PM? I'll be back from work by then.*"

"That works for me," Penelope agreed.

Bridget returned indoors and later reappeared at the door, handing Penelope a piece of paper with a phone number. Penelope glanced at the number, then tucked the crumpled paper into her handbag and bid farewell. Descending the stairs, Penelope contemplated Bridget's role. She considered the likelihood that Bridget could only provide the company's name if the landlord was involved in a corporate rental agreement. Penelope dismissed the possibility that the previous tenant shared the same company with Bridget, reasoning that if they did, Bridget would likely have known or at least had some information about them. As she reached the gate, her waiting cab awaited her, and she stepped in, heading back to her own place.

From then on, her primary concern shifted to tracking down the man from her dreams. Even during the cab ride home, her mind was consumed by thoughts of how to effectively pursue that single lead. Bridget's offer marked a promising start, and Penelope eagerly anticipated the moment she would make that pivotal call.

That evening, Penelope contacted Christine to explain her absence from their usual meeting and shared details of the previous night's dream. She described how she had followed Christine's suggestion of focusing on clues, and she expressed her gratitude for Christine's perceptive understanding of the dreams.

Feeling mentally drained from her day of contemplation, Penelope retired to bed early. Upon waking the following morning, she yearned for time to pass swiftly. Her sole desire was to receive information that would propel her forward. For the first time, she wished hours could compress into mere seconds or minutes, as the 8 PM call time felt too distant.

Throughout most of the morning, Penelope remained in bed, consumed by thoughts of the impending call. She occupied herself with reading, momentarily distracting herself from her persistent dreams. Around 11 AM, hunger drove her to the kitchen, where she prepared a meal before returning to bed to continue reading. Eventually, she drifted into slumber and awoke three hours later, perspiring and teary-eyed.

The intense heat of the sun, now on the western side of the building, permeated her room through the lace curtains. The sun's rays acted like voracious demons, draining moisture from her body with invisible needles and syringes. As tears streamed down her face, Penelope recalled another dream, this time filled with her questions and pleas. She questioned the man's love for her, his disappearances, and his treatment of her. Her words were punctuated by sobs as she poured out her emotions.

The man, who had appeared in her dream, heard every word clearly and was moved by her heartfelt expressions. He rose from his seat by the bedside, walked to the window, and glanced back at Penelope, clearly troubled by her words. After a moment of contemplation, he returned to the other side of the bed and stood behind her, facing her as she lay on her side, facing the window.

"I hate seeing you like this, and I'm not who you think I am. Please, just listen to me," the man pleaded with Penelope, seeing her tears.

As his words reached her, Penelope turned to face him, feeling overwhelmed by his presence. She stopped crying almost instantly upon hearing his voice.

"This will be the last time you see me," the man declared. Confused, Penelope asked, *"What do you mean?"*

"I've realized that I can't provide what you need, and I didn't anticipate that my love and actions would cause you so much pain. It hurts me to see you cry like this because I can't fulfil your desires. It would be selfish of me to continue this. That's why I've decided to end it," he explained.

Penelope interrupted, her voice trembling, *"Why are you leaving? Can't we have a normal relationship if you truly love me?"*

"Believe me, I'm doing this for your well-being. If you care about me, please go to..." he provided her with an address.

"Promise me, just this one last time. Do it for us," he pleaded, and after a brief pause, Penelope responded firmly, *"I promise."*

The man held Penelope's left hand in a gesture of apology and comfort. Slowly, he began to fade away as Penelope implored him not to disappear. Overwhelmed with emotion, Penelope cried out, and suddenly, she woke up.

Later that day, Penelope contacted her friends and informed them she would be joining their regular gathering. During the meeting, she recounted everything, starting from her visit to the apartment and detailing the dream from that afternoon. Surprisingly, even Edith was at a loss for words this time, attentively listening to Penelope's story from beginning to end without interruption.

"Wow, so what are you going to do?" Edith asked.

"What's your advice?" Penelope inquired.

The Virtues of Split Personality

"I suggest you honour your promise and go there as soon as possible. Are you still on leave?" Edith questioned.

"Yes, I have this entire week off. I'll be back at work next Monday," Penelope replied.

"Then this is the perfect opportunity. You could travel tomorrow or even the day after. Utilize your short leave and return, let's say... on Sunday, so you can be back for work on Monday," Edith advised.

"I think Edith has a point. You might not get another chance to go so soon after this week," Christine chimed in.

Penelope hesitated, considering her options. *"Do you think I should wait?"* she pondered.

"Something else might come up, like him appearing in another dream," Penelope added.

"I doubt that. If he did return, it might be to scold you for not keeping your promise," Edith remarked.

"Besides, you still have that phone call to make in the evening. You never know where that could lead you," Christine added.

Penelope felt torn, uncertain about her friends' seemingly definitive advice.

"Why don't you give us a call once you've heard from Bridget?" Christine suggested with a knowing smile.

"Though I don't expect any improvement from what he's already conveyed in your last dream," she added.

"I'm not in a rush to head home, and I'd be happy to accompany you and help you decide your next step after the call," Edith offered.

"Count me in as well," Christine chimed in, joining Edith's offer.

The three friends headed to Penelope's place together. At 8 PM, Penelope made the call to Bridget. While Bridget provided the landlord's name, she mentioned that her company hadn't been the previous renter of the flat. She informed Penelope that the person who had given her the information wasn't entirely certain about the company and promised to provide more details later.

With incomplete information in hand, Edith became even more persuasive, urging Penelope to take the trip. "Furthermore, the company she mentioned is right here. You can follow up even after your leave ends if the trip doesn't yield results," Edith reasoned.

"When did you become so insightful?" Christine playfully asked.

The Virtues of Split Personality

Edith smiled and replied, *"I can't wait to see where all this leads to. It could either end terribly or beautifully.*" Christine pressed further, *"Are you saying you don't care how it ends?"*

Edith's tone softened as she reassured Penelope,

"Ultimately, I do want a positive outcome, but I promise I'll stand by you regardless."

She extended her arm, touching Penelope's shoulder, and continued,

"If it turns out the way you're hoping, I'll be equally thrilled. I just want you to have your life back. This dream ordeal has consumed you, and we haven't been able to spend quality time together. It's been either you alone trying to solve this mystery or us together discussing the same thing."

"I understand your concern, and I'm grateful for it. However, we can't predict when this will come to an end," Penelope responded, appreciating her friends' support.

"That's why we're here, together we'll put an end to this. Make the trip while you still have a few days on your leave. If it doesn't work out there, we can follow up on the company when you return," Edith asserted with determination.

"But I have a small problem," Penelope interjected.

"What's that?" Christine inquired.

"I don't have enough money," Penelope admitted.

I'll help you out with some funds. Let me know your budget," Edith offered.

"I'll contribute too," Christine chimed in.

"Mind you, mine isn't a contribution. I'll figure it out how to get my money back once you're back from the trip. I'm not that nice," Edith added with a smirk.

Penelope and Christine exchanged glances and rolled their eyes in response to Edith's remark.

"Okay, okay, I can't be generous without some strategy, think what you like," Edith teased, catching onto their silent exchange.

As Christine and Edith departed, the plan was set, Penelope would travel on Friday. With only a day to prepare, Penelope focused on getting ready.

The evening before her departure, Penelope lay naked on her bed, reflecting on her graduation photos. The past two weeks had stirred a feeling within her a longing for a normal life, one filled with love and companionship. She envisioned a real relationship with a man who genuinely cared for her. Memories of Jack brought irritation and frustration; he was nothing like the man in her dreams, the one she was about to pursue.

Her thoughts became heavy; a mix of fear and apprehension filled the room. She felt the need to shower, sweat collecting on her forehead and body. She pondered her connection with the mysterious man, wondering how she had managed to evade other men's advances but not his. She questioned his tactic of invading her dreams, wondering if Edith was somehow involved.

This surreal experience had been overwhelming, and Penelope had sought solace in sharing her ordeal with Edith and Christine. Their support and ideas had provided relief, allowing her to offload her burden.

In two days, she would embark on her journey, hoping to find answers and closure. As she left her bed and headed to the shower, her dressing mirror seemed to beckon her, reflecting the qualities she admired in herself. She applied cold water, feeling the initial sting before it began to invigorate her.

Her mind wandered, recalling the stranger's touch on her breasts. She managed to snap out of her reverie, wondering if he had somehow entered her reality. Reassured she was alone, Penelope continued her shower, feeling refreshed as she stepped out.

Naked, she began packing for the trip. Alone in her own space, she considered her encounter with the man and the impression she wanted to make. With determination, Penelope prepared herself for the inevitable, aiming for a positive outcome.

Chapter 15

Christopher slammed the phone down onto its receiver, exclaiming in frustration, *"Good grief! Where is he?"* He angrily questioned, then swiftly picked up the phone again to connect with his personal secretary.

"Cindy, reach out to Arthur and request his presence here," he *instructed.*

Cindy was taken aback by the intensity in her boss's voice. She internally reminded herself to handle the task with utmost urgency, not wanting to face potential consequences.

Recently, she had observed her boss's mood becoming increasingly erratic. This change had emerged following his return from his time off. On occasion, he would become subdued and withdrawn, while at other times he would explode into unwarranted fits of anger, directing his outbursts at both colleagues and subordinates. Surprisingly, his behaviour was met with patience and understanding from those around him. Everyone had become aware of the tragic loss of his twin brother, recognizing that he was grappling with the difficult process of acceptance.

Patson M. Chifumbe

Cindy contacted the drivers' pool office and requested Arthur's presence in Mr. Wright's office. Arthur was the dependable driver of the company, characterized by his substantial build and thick Mustache that gave him the appearance of an overweight wrestler. His towering height set him apart from the rest of the staff, although his colleagues affectionately referred to him as the *'Hulk.'*

Upon entering the office, a familiar voice addressed Arthur, asking, *"Where is Carmelo?"* The tone in Christopher's voice sent a shiver down Arthur's spine, freezing him in place as he stared at his boss with wide-open eyes. In the midst of that formal setting, Arthur's mind went blank.

"I'm not sure, sir," he eventually managed to respond when he found his voice.

"It's been an hour since lunch break, and he hasn't returned to his office. Please check on him at his home. We have a meeting on Monday, and he hasn't provided me with necessary information. If possible, bring him here or retrieve a diskette containing the third quarter financial report. I need to review it over the weekend. I've been trying to reach him on his cell phone, but it's unreachable. I can't believe he expects me to contribute to

The Virtues of Split Personality

the meeting without reviewing that report. What an ineffective board secretary."

Carmelo, as the senior accountant, reported to the CFO. Christopher had recently been promoted to Chief Financial Officer, but surprisingly, this elevation hadn't calmed his fragile emotions.

This was the second time Arthur had encountered Christopher in such a sour mood within the week. Arthur almost rushed out of the office to retrieve the diskette or Carmelo himself.

Christopher hadn't confided in anyone about another matter troubling him. It was the frustration of his personal life, particularly his romantic life, amidst all the chaos. He felt incredibly lonely. Ever since the incident involving Catherine during their school days, Christopher had never been involved in a romantic relationship. His interactions with women were limited to paid encounters with prostitutes. This wasn't his preferred path, but he felt compelled to find relief in that manner since he was rejected by respectable women. He longed to find someone to share his life with, to settle down, and to start a family of his own. His attempts at proposing had always resulted in uncomfortable discussions about his past, which didn't improve his situation. Consequently, he had given up on pursuing that avenue.

Despite his brother's recent passing, which was equally painful, Christopher had hoped that this aspect of his life might eventually change. While he wasn't enthusiastic about it, the thought did cross his mind.

Chapter 16

Penelope boarded the 8 a.m. bus, embarking on a journey lasting six hours that ended in New Orleans by 2 p.m. The experience proved to be her most unpleasant voyage, primarily due to her anxiety about the unknown ahead and how she would navigate it. Upon reaching her destination, Penelope promptly decided to purchase a detailed town map to aid her exploration. She was determined not to reveal any uncertainties about her directions. After disembarking, she inquired about a map and received directions to shops specializing in tourist items across the street. Once she acquired the map, she studied it and easily located her desired road. The next step was to find a taxi. Spotting a fleet of taxis a short walk away from where she was, she navigated through the crowded corridors, inadvertently drawing the attention of some men. Unbeknownst to her, one of them found her quite attractive and wondered about her relationship status.

He gazed at her with jealousy, envying the fortunate man in her life. How incredibly lucky that guy must be! Why do some men have all the luck? What would it take for me to be with someone like her?

Penelope carried only a small black bag, suggesting she wasn't embarking on a long journey. The guy assumed she might be one of those who parked their cars nearby. He couldn't take his eyes off her, and when she hailed a taxi, he eagerly seized the opportunity. Hurrying toward her, he greeted me, *"Hello there,"* and she inquired if he was a cab driver.

Penelope asked, *"Could you please take me to my destination? I'm headed to Lansdale Street in Avis. Are you familiar with the route?"*
"Absolutely, Miss. You're in good hands. No need to worry. I know his town inside out, just like the back of my hand. We'll reach there before you know it," he assured her.

Despite the guy's somewhat disheveled appearance, Penelope found his confidence impressive. *"Great, I don't want any complications,"* she thought. He walked a few steps ahead, circled around a taxi, and opened the passenger-side front door. Assuming it was his car, Penelope politely declined, stating, *"Thank you, but I'd prefer to sit in the back."*

The guy closed the front door and opened the rear one. Making his own mark on Penelope, he held the door for her, revealing a grin that showed off his gold canine tooth. Penelope thanked him and settled into the back seat. Before they set off, she inquired about the cost of the journey. He explained two options: a fare based on the distance using a meter or a fixed agreed-upon amount. After pondering, Penelope chose the metered option, intending to test her bargaining skills with the other choice next time.

The taxi driver started the engine, and they began their drive. Ten minutes later, they veered onto Lansdale Street. The driver noticed the meter had stopped running for the first time and informed Penelope. Curious, she asked, *"So, does that mean you can provide me with the fare upfront, since only one option remains?"*

The driver took a moment to respond, during which Penelope thought he was considering a fair price. *"It's $70.00,"* he eventually stated.

"What? That's too expensive," Penelope exclaimed.

The cab driver abruptly pulled over by the roadside and ordered, *"Get out,"* which caught Penelope off guard. Puzzled, she questioned his actions, to which he responded firmly, *"I'm going back."*

Shocked, Penelope protested, *"You can't do this! You're supposed to take me to my final destination."*

His response was cut: *"Watch me."*

With the road empty, he accelerated, covering around 50 meters before veering onto a dusty road leading to a farmhouse about 5 kilometres away from Lansdale Street. Racing at a reckless 120 mph on the uneven gravel, Penelope was tossed violently within the car, desperately pleading for him to stop. The car came to an abrupt halt, shrouded in a cloud of dust that resembled a whirlwind from a distance.

After the dust settled slightly, the driver emerged and opened the back door. He seized Penelope by her right arm and forcibly dragged her out. She didn't resist, relieved to escape the car, although he handled her roughly, causing her to fall to the ground. Her right hip made contact with the pebble-covered road first, prompting a slight groan. The driver let go of her arm, snatched her small bag from her left hand, and hastily rummaged through it.

Distracted by the honking of an approaching car, he abruptly halted his actions. As the car pulled up, he quickly returned to his cab and sped away from the scene.

"Are you alright, Miss?" her rescuer asked with concern.

"I believe so," Penelope replied, picking herself up, dusting off her jeans and retrieving her bag.

"What happened there?" The Good Samaritan inquired.

"I suspect that guy was on drugs," Penelope explained, briefly sharing the details of her ordeal.

Despite needing to continue to his own destination, the man offered his assistance. He suggested that if Penelope was comfortable with the idea, she could accompany him to a farmhouse at the end of the gravel road. He needed to meet one of his bosses there. Seeing a flicker of unease cross her face, he understood that his suggestion might not have been well-received. Given what she had just experienced, he realized his proposal might not have been appropriate. He reconsidered, thinking, "Maybe it wasn't the best idea after all. Who could blame her?"

Apologizing, he said, *"I'm sorry if that came across as insensitive. So, where were you originally headed?"*

"I'm visiting a friend at Cappello flats in Avis," Penelope responded.

"Cappello flats? I'm familiar with them. One of our managers resides there, the same person who sent me on this errand. Luckily, it's not far from here. How about we take you there first, and then I can return for my business?"

"Please, that would be incredibly kind," Penelope gratefully accepted, a genuine smile lighting up her face.

They swiftly hopped into the car and executed a U-turn. Within a brief five-minute span, the car pulled up outside the flats. Penelope turned to the driver and expressed her gratitude.

"You have no idea how thankful I am," she admitted, revealing her unique situation. *"Believe it or not, I've never met the person I'm here to visit."*

"Are you saying you're not from around here?" the man inquired.

"Yes, that's correct," Penelope confirmed.

"In that case, why don't you find out if this person is present? I'll

wait. *Just give me a signal if everything's okay,*" the man proposed.

"*Thank you so much. Your thoughtfulness means a lot, and I might still need your assistance,*" Penelope responded, genuinely touched by his offer.

Full of appreciation, Penelope exited the car and entered the complex through its gate. After some time ringing the doorbell of her intended destination, a lady emerged on the balcony – her next-door neighbour. After a quick assessment, the neighbour opened the grill gate and engaged Penelope in conversation.

"*It's likely there's no one inside, and Mr. Wright is probably still at work,*" the neighbour informed Penelope. "*Are you one of his sisters?*" she inquired.

"*No, not at all,*" Penelope answered honestly.

"*Are you a local?*" the neighbour continued her questioning.

"*No, actually I just arrived in town about an hour ago. My name is Penelope,*" she replied.

"*Well, since it's Friday, I'd recommend trying to reach him at his workplace before he finishes. You know how bachelors tend to go out and come back late on Fridays,*" the neighbour suggested.

"Do you happen to know where he works?" Penelope asked.

"*No,*" she admitted.

"*Just ask the taxi driver to take you to Barclays main branch right in the town centre,*" the neighbour offered.

The memory of her recent unsettling encounter with a taxi driver flooded Penelope's mind. She felt relieved that the man who had brought her there was waiting for her. She silently prayed that he would still be willing to assist her.

"*Of course he would, that's why he offered to wait for the outcome,*" a voice in the back of Penelope's mind reassured her.

"*By the way, I'm sorry if I seemed nosy; it's just that I rarely see any women coming to inquire about him,*" the neighbour explained.

"*That's perfectly fine, and thank you very much for your help,*" Penelope responded, making her way down the stairs.

A short while later, the man spotted Penelope walking back towards the car. "How did it go? Did you find him?" he inquired.

"*The neighbour told me he's at work,*" Penelope replied.

"*And where exactly is that?*" the man asked, curiously.

"*He works at Barclays bank, right in the centre of town,*" Penelope answered.

The man thoughtfully guessed, "*That must be my boss. Why did you have to travel all this way when you could have found him in town?*" he questioned further.

"*You're right to ask, and you must be wondering about the whole situation. It's quite a story,*" Penelope admitted.

"*I hate to pry, but I have a feeling I might know who you're looking for,*" the man ventured.

"*Feel free to share. You've already been so kind to me. Who knows, you might be able to save me a lot of trouble with all of this,*" Penelope responded.

Curious, the man asked, "*What's his name?*"

"*Mr. Wright,*" Penelope revealed.

"*Yes, that's him. He's my boss,*" the man declared triumphantly. "*Hop in, and let's find a cab to take you there.*"

"*Wait, you work with him, don't you?*" Penelope questioned.

"*Yes,*" the man confirmed.

"*May I ask where you were initially headed to?*" Penelope probed.

"To see another one of my bosses at a farmhouse at the end of that gravel road," the man replied.

"And then you're heading back to the office?" Penelope inquired for confirmation.

"Yes, indeed," the man affirmed.

"Tell you what, forget about the cab. How would you feel about having a somewhat miserable company with me? Honestly, I feel safe with you," Penelope proposed.

The man seemed like an angel sent to her, and she didn't hold back her gratitude.

"Be my guest," the man graciously accepted, and they drove away.

As they neared the open gate of the farmhouse, they spotted someone seated on the veranda. Moments later, they parked in front of the house. Carmelo, topless with a can of Heineken beside him, appeared to be temporarily drowning his sorrows, according to Arthur's observations.

Arthur was privy to Carmelo's personal issues, including his infidelity case. He knew why Carmelo had ended up at this new residence. Carmelo's wife had kicked him out of their home, and he was on probation, allowed to return only if he reformed and proved his remorse. Seeing the car drive in, Carmelo assumed that only Arthur would show up. He stood up, brushing off his clothes, secretly hoping it was his wife coming to take him back from his difficult situation.

As Arthur parked the car, Carmelo realized that the woman accompanying Arthur was not his wife. Arthur got out of the car and walked over to his boss.

"Arthur, what brings you here?" Carmelo inquired.

"Mr. Wright was waiting for you to brief him on next week's meeting. When he realized you might not make it, he sent me to fetch the diskette with the financial quarterly report from you, if you wouldn't come with me," Arthur explained.

"Damn, I completely forgot about that. It's in my briefcase. Let me retrieve it for you," Carmelo said, disappearing into the house and returning with a folded envelope, which he handed to Arthur.

"Apologize to him on my behalf." Carmelo then took a couple of steps closer to Arthur and in a hushed tone asked,

"Who's the woman with you in the car?" He motioned towards the car.

"Oh, her. She's Mr. Wright's guest," Arthur responded.

Arthur added, *"Bad idea, bad idea, Carmelo. We don't know who might have seen you here, and they could assume you're bringing women for me. Do you want to become my accomplice?"*

"Oh my God, I never even thought of that. I apologize, sir," Arthur responded, feeling genuinely remorseful.

"See you on Monday, Arthur," Carmelo said, dismissing him after handing over the diskette.

Carmelo was typically a cheerful and sociable man, known as the life of the company. But from that brief encounter, Arthur could sense that he must have been deeply offended. His depression seemed to be surfacing. Carmelo was likely missing his wife and children greatly, Arthur thought.

Chapter 17

As Arthur and Penelope returned to the town, their conversation was limited, mostly revolving around Penelope's journey. In quiet contemplation, they reflected on the events of the day, and eventually, they arrived in front of the bank.

"Here we are," Arthur announced, glancing at Penelope.

Observing the imposing building partially obscured by the car's roof, Penelope read the inscription above the entrance: "BARCLAYS BANK MAIN BRANCH." She gazed at the long set of stairs leading to the structure, narrowing as they ascended and converging onto a white terrazzo floor before two glass doors. The ground floor's walls were constructed from glossy black marble.

Are you alright?" Arthur inquired. Caught in a distant reverie, Penelope replied, *"Oh, yes."*

She had slipped into one of those distant, detached states of mind. Arthur had often felt he was on the brink of a fantasy, a story teetering on the edge of reality. He marvelled at how a seemingly intelligent and beautiful young woman like Penelope

The Virtues of Split Personality

had embarked on a journey fraught with uncertainties. Such an endeavour demanded courage and determination, he thought.

"I'll need to go around and park the car. You can head to the reception, and someone there will guide you to his office."

Expressing gratitude for Arthur's assistance, Penelope exited the car and surveyed the towering building. Its architecture appeared to lean towards her, defying gravity while remaining steadfast. With resolve, Penelope ascended the lengthy staircase and eventually arrived at the reception area.

"Hello, I would like to meet with Mr. Wright," Penelope stated.
"Mr. Christopher Wright?" the receptionist clarified.
"Yes, the one residing in Avis."
"Indeed, that's him," the receptionist affirmed.
"Head to the tenth floor, go to the third door on your right, which belongs to his secretary," she indicated, pointing towards the elevators.
"Thank you very much," Penelope expressed her gratitude.
"You're welcome," replied the receptionist, her gaze following Penelope until she entered one of the elevators.

The Virtues of Split Personality

It wasn't common for clients, especially women of Penelope's age and beauty, to be so pleasant when seeking assistance. Most would gather information and promptly leave. Upon reaching the designated floor, Penelope followed the directions, arriving at the third door after a few steps. Taking a deep breath, she knocked on the closed door, waited for permission, and then introduced herself while requesting to see Mr. Wright. The secretary directed her to a seat, explaining that someone was still inside.

After a while, the individual exited, prompting Penelope to enter after another knock. However, her movement halted abruptly as she entered, shocked by the sight of the man seated behind the table. A moment of wordless mutual amazement passed between Penelope and Mr. Wright.

"Is there a problem?" the secretary inquired, addressing Penelope.

Penelope didn't respond, causing the secretary to rise from her chair and approach her.

"Miss," she gently touched Penelope's shoulder. Only then did Penelope snap out of her trance and

continue walking inside, still in disbelief.

"Sir, is everything okay?" the secretary questioned.

"I suppose so, and thank you for asking," Mr. Wright finally responded.

His gaze remained fixed on Penelope as he spoke. The secretary retreated to her office, shutting the door behind her. Her boss's personal life had been confined to his family photos on his desk, leaving her to speculate that what she had just witnessed might signify the arrival of a past lover. As she closed the door, this thought lingered in her mind.

Penelope stood motionless for a while before being offered a seat. In her mind, she thought, "I have found him, this is him." Christopher managed to regain his composure and extended an apology, admitting his unusual behaviour. He recognized that he had acted like someone who had been isolated for years and was encountering a woman for the first time.

As he shuffled through papers on his desk, he inquired,

"Yes please, may I help you?" In her hopeful anticipation,

The Virtues of Split Personality

Penelope wished his initial words would alleviate the situation, perhaps with sentiments like, *"Is it truly you? I'm this moment."* However, what she heard was a plain, *"Yes please, may I help you?"*

Those words caused Penelope to take a step back, leaving her speechless and overwhelmed. She felt an immense weight on her chest, struggling to breathe. Sitting down, she shook her head from side to side, unable to hold back her emotions. Tears streamed down her face as she buried her head in her hands and sobbed. Christopher was taken aback, unsure of how to react. He rose from his seat but remained still behind his desk, grappling with the situation.

Numerous thoughts raced through his mind, leading him to the conclusion that his innocence was crucial. He signalled for his secretary to join them and bring a glass of water.

> *"What's the matter, sir?"* The secretary inquired upon her arrival.
> *"She hasn't uttered a word since she entered,"* he replied, his concern evident.

Patson M. Chifumbe

When the secretary entered, Penelope felt as though she had become a burden and managed to regain control over her emotions. She glanced at the secretary, who was now beside her, and extended her hand to accept the glass of water. Meanwhile, Arthur walked into the secretary's office, only to find her absent. He knocked on the boss's door and hesitated upon seeing the secretary, the boss, and the lady he had dropped off earlier. However, the boss gestured for him to enter. Holding a folded envelope, Arthur approached the boss's table, extending his arm across it to hand over the envelope. As he did, he noticed Penelope's tearful state, leaving both the boss and the secretary astonished. Emotions had finally overwhelmed her, a stark contrast to her demeaner since Arthur had picked her up after the incident. Arthur had assumed she was remarkably strong not to have displayed any emotional breakdown until now.

Arthur requested a private conversation with his boss in another room. Christopher left his desk and joined Arthur in the secretary's office. Expecting some message from Carmelo, Christopher was taken aback when Arthur revealed that he had brought Penelope to the office and shared the circumstances of how they had met.

The Virtues of Split Personality

"I'm not sure what's happening, but thank you very much," Mr. Wright expressed before returning to his office, and Arthur departed.

After their brief discussion, Christopher grasped the reason behind Penelope's emotional outpouring, and he felt a sense of compassion for her. Yet, he still pondered why she had undertaken the journey to seek him out.

"I apologize; my confusion got the best of me, and I didn't expect to break down like this," Penelope confessed.

"Are you sure everything is alright, Miss?" the secretary inquired.

"Please, don't worry. I assure you, I'm perfectly fine," Penelope reassured.

"Well, it's time for me to leave for the day. I hope you won't need me, sir," the secretary remarked.

"We hope not," Mr. Wright replied, his gaze shifting from the secretary to Penelope. Their eyes locked momentarily.

"See you on Monday, sir, and goodbye, ma'am," the secretary bid farewell, exiting the room and closing the door behind her.

Seated in his chair, Mr. Wright addressed Penelope, asking,

Patson M. Chifumbe

"*So, madam, how can I assist you?*"

"*It's a personal matter, and I'm not entirely sure how you can help me,*" Penelope replied. "*I arrived in town about three hours ago and immediately went to your home using the directions I was given. Unfortunately, no one was there, but your neighbour mentioned you were at work.*"

"*Please, go on,*" Mr. Wright urged, prompting Penelope to continue explaining her reason for seeking him out.

Penelope took a moment before responding to his question about her confusion. She checked her watch, realizing it was past quitting time. "*Why don't you help me find a place to stay?* I could use a shower after such a long day. Afterward, I can share everything over a meal. If I were to delve into the details now, it might take an hour or more, and I believe time is not on our side here," Penelope proposed.

"*Well, if you're comfortable with that, I have no objections,*" Mr. Wright agreed.

A short while later, they exited the building. Christopher led the way, carrying Penelope's small bag over his shoulder and

The Virtues of Split Personality

his briefcase in his hand. They walked to his car, parked in the bank's parking lot. As they drove away, Christopher suggested stopping at his place first to change into something casual and leave his briefcase. The drive was mostly silent, punctuated by glances exchanged between them. Soon, they arrived at Christopher's residence.

"By the way, you're welcome to use the shower here, if you don't mind," Christopher offered as he parked the car at the flats.
"That's perfectly fine with me, and I could really use it," Penelope replied.

As they both reached for the bag and briefcase simultaneously while Christopher turned off the engine, their faces came close. Frozen in that moment, their eyes met and locked. Penelope saw Mr. Wright's pupils dilate, a sensation reminiscent of her dreams. Likewise, Christopher was captivated by her beauty. He withdrew, apologizing, and licked his lips nervously.

"Oh my God," Penelope audibly exclaimed upon witnessing this.
"Is something wrong?" Mr. Wright inquired, but

Penelope remained silent. She recalled him doing the same gesture in one of her dreams.

Exiting the car with her belongings, Penelope closed the door using her knee and Christopher retrieved her bag and briefcase. Inside the flat, he placed her bag on the couch and directed her to the shower room while he headed to his bedroom. After collecting some items from her bag, Penelope returned to the living room. In his bedroom, Christopher stored his briefcase in the wardrobe and removed his jacket. He then sprawled on his bed, staring at the ceiling, pondering the identity and intentions of the woman before him. Overwhelmed by her beauty, he whispered, *"Who is this lady, and what does she want?"*

As if remembering something, he swiftly got up and returned to the living room just as Penelope was preparing to head to the bathroom. He rubbed his hands together and asked, "You might want to change your clothes. Do you need anything ironed?"

"Yes, my dress," Penelope replied.

"I could be of assistance. Let me iron it for you and hang it in the passage when I'm done," Christopher offered.

Penelope retrieved her bag, passing it to him, and thanked him. *"It's my pleasure,"* Christopher responded. *"Tea, coffee, what would you like before we have our meal?"*

"Tea," she answered before heading to the bathroom.

In her mind, Penelope searched for answers. *"It's him,"* she thought.

"But why doesn't he seem to remember me?" She questioned herself.

After some time, Penelope emerged from the bathroom, her long black hair clinging to her skin and emphasizing her beautiful features. Christopher had stepped out of the room to give her privacy. Eventually, she reappeared in her dress, which fit her perfectly as if tailor-made. Christopher playfully mused to himself, *"She really is a designer human being."*

His growing feelings for her were becoming overwhelming, driving him to the brink. She seemed even more captivating with every glance, leaving him unsure of what to do next.

As Christopher finished preparing tea, Penelope entered the room and offered her assistance. He declined, saying, *"Actually, I'm done. Just make yourself comfortable."*

Moments later, he brought the tea and biscuits to the table on a tray. They briefly discussed the neighbour's assumption that Penelope was Christopher's sister and delved into bachelors' lifestyles, particularly on the weekends.

"She even suggested I follow you to your workplace, just in case you didn't come straight home," Penelope shared.
"I find it hard to believe she said that," Christopher remarked.
"What's wrong with that?" Penelope inquired.
"The impression she's given you is that I'm a night owl," he explained.
"That's common knowledge, and for a moment, I saw myself and couldn't agree with her more," Penelope replied.

As their conversation continued, Christopher's feelings for Penelope continued to grow stronger.

"So, now that I know you're single, what do you do?" Christopher inquired, using the question as a segue into deeper personal conversation.

The Virtues of Split Personality

"I'm a trainee at a marketing company. I completed my Advertising Diploma last year," Penelope replied.

"Very beautiful," he commented, his gaze fixed on her. It was unclear whether he was referring to her answer or her as a person.

During their exchange, Penelope took the opportunity to survey the layout of the kitchen, dining, and living room. The space formed an *"L"* shape, with the kitchen on one short side, the dining area at a right angle in the middle, and the living room along the longer side of the *"L."* The entrance into the flat led between the living and dining areas. A corridor opposite the entrance led to the bedroom, bathroom, and toilet. Penelope's eyes eventually landed on a large portrait of Christopher on the wall at the far end of the room. Flanking it were two smaller portraits that weren't entirely clear from her vantage point. Intrigued, she got up from her chair and approached the portraits for a closer look.

"It seems you're quite fond of yourself," Penelope remarked.

"Why?" Christopher questioned.

"The portraits, they suggest that no one else deserves a spot on the wall but you," she playfully pointed out.

The Virtues of Split Personality

Patson M. Chifumbe

Christopher responded, "Not necessarily. I'd be more than happy to put yours up there if you gave me one." Penelope smiled at the remark, recognizing his intention to impress her whenever he could.

"Unfortunately, I don't have any with me right now," Penelope replied.

"Too bad for me," Christopher responded with a grin, eliciting another smile from Penelope.

"By the way, that's me in the large portrait, and in one of the smaller ones. The other small one is my brother," Christopher explained.

"You mean you're a twin?" Penelope asked.

"Yes," he confirmed.

Penelope felt like she had stumbled upon a significant piece of information.

"So where is he?" she inquired.

"Unfortunately, he passed away about a month ago," Christopher revealed.

The Virtues of Split Personality

Penelope's stomach knotted as she absorbed the news. She sank onto the couch, supporting her head with her left hand, her gaze fixed on the floor. The sudden revelation disoriented her. Questions swirled in her mind, yet Christopher remained silent, offering no answers. After collecting herself, she managed to articulate her question, *"What happened?"*

Christopher, sensing her distress, stood up from the dining chair he was seated on, walked to the living room, and retrieved a tape from his collection. He switched on the television and video deck, inserting the tape. He then settled on the couch opposite Penelope. She was puzzled by his actions, expecting an answer instead. "Did you get my question, or do you not want to talk about it?" Penelope inquired.

"I did, and please watch, but I'm warning you, it's not a pleasant thing to see," Christopher cautioned.

The tape began, showing the convertible Audi passing the lady on the street, and the driver turning to look at her. As the recording reached the point of the accident, Penelope mentioned that it was in her hometown of New Orleans. "I was there," she stated. The scene played out, and Penelope recalled the incident. She had been one of the onlookers who had continued on their way after the accident. She requested to see the scene again.

Just as the car passed the lady, Penelope asked Christopher to pause the tape. With a quivering voice and tears welling up, she exclaimed, *"That's me."*

"He was looking at me," she added.

Christopher replayed the tape in slow motion, confirming that it was indeed her, and his brother had been looking at her. By the end of the video, Penelope was sobbing, her body shaking with emotion. *"It's me. He died because of me,"* she murmured.

Christopher was taken aback, comprehending the tragic connection. He deduced that his brother had been captivated by Penelope's beauty, which had led to the accident. The memories of his brother flooded his mind, and tears streamed down his cheeks. He turned off the television and video deck, removing the tape. They both sat in silence until Penelope began to share her dreams, leading up to her arrival. Christopher couldn't hold back his tears as he listened.

Overwhelmed by the revelation, he moved to sit beside her, no longer able to contain his emotions. He realized he couldn't blame her, considering they had never met before. Moreover, his brother seemed to have guided her to him. A sense of responsibility filled his heart, compelling him to fulfil his brother's wishes. He vowed not to let his departed brother down again.

Taking Penelope's left hand in his, he spoke, *"We had the same name. It was my grandfather's idea. He found it challenging and interesting, according to him."*

"He said, 'Life without anything to think about is a waste and boring. And if one's life is without challenges, then it must be a very dull life. One should always have something worthwhile to do but, of course, should be mindful not to cause trouble. Anyone who loves trouble finds trouble, and that is no way to live life. Challenges in one's daily life enrich the mind and equip one with survival instincts. Such a person would be able to handle most of these daily hurdles, more than someone who has the same routine life. With a routine life, anything different would be a source of headache,'" Christopher shared with

The Virtues of Split Personality

Penelope.

He continued, recounting their school days and how they eventually went their separate ways, leaving out the incident involving Catherine as he found it too embarrassing to discuss.

> "In fact, it was much later that we learned the old man was also behind what transpired, due to his concerns about something that he believed was affecting our lives and potentially damaging the family name,"

Christopher explained.

Chapter 18

The sequence of events took a different turn, altering the entire situation. Suddenly, they were no longer hungry; the sensation of hunger had vanished.

"There's no need for us to search for accommodations elsewhere. You can stay here for the night. After all, you're my guest, aren't you?" Christopher concluded his firm statement with a question.

Penelope remained silent. Christopher stood up from the sofa and proceeded to the bedroom. After a while, he returned to the living room.

"Are you okay?" he inquired.

"How could I be okay? This is overwhelming for me. Why is this happening to me?" she replied with her own question.

Christopher stayed quiet. He wondered if he would have shown the same level of affection his brother had for Penelope in a similar situation. He thought to himself that his brother must have been captivated by Penelope's beauty and temporarily lost sight of his surroundings.

Patson M. Chifumbe

"I've arranged your sleeping area. I hope you don't mind sharing the same room. You'll have the bed, and I've placed an extra mattress on the floor next to the bed for myself," he explained.

Christopher's decision was influenced by the overwhelming and somewhat terrifying nature of the revelation. He believed that sharing the same room would help alleviate Penelope's fear. *"Please go rest. I'll wash the cups and join you shortly,"* Christopher said, his tone sounding more like a request than a command.

Penelope got up from the sofa and headed to the bedroom.

The next morning, Christopher woke up early. His feelings from the previous day toward the woman who had unexpectedly entered his life remained unchanged. *"Yes, walked into my life. She knew what she was doing. She knew exactly what she would find,"* he thought to himself.

He convinced himself that the feelings were mutual, which explained her presence. He rose from the mattress on the floor where he had spent a restless night. It had been a night devoid of sleep. Throughout the dark hours, he wished for time to speed up

The Virtues of Split Personality

so he could catch a glimpse of the woman sleeping in his bed as soon as daylight arrived.

Upon waking, his gaze lingered on her face, partially hidden by the beddings, with a hint of desire before he headed to the shower. After bathing, Christopher dressed neatly and casually. He wore a maroon pullover with a zipper, black tailored cotton slacks from 'Serioes,' and black strap saddles. The trousers had been a gift from his grandfather, who had purchased them in Luanshya, Zambia, and Christopher had always appreciated their comfort. He had inherited a natural scent from his grandfather and didn't feel the need for sprays or deodorants. A memory of his grandfather's advice about women's appearances crossed his mind.

In the kitchen, he hastily devised a romantic reason to wake Penelope. He prepared warm milk and approached the bedroom with the glass in hand. Christopher hoped his grandfather's wisdom wouldn't disrupt his growing affection for her. Penelope stirred as she felt a touch on her leg. Facing upwards, she saw Christopher holding a glass of milk.

"Good morning," he greeted.

Sitting up against the headboard, she rubbed her eyes and acknowledged him. Christopher was delighted to see Penelope's natural appearance, untouched by makeup. He handed her the milk, appreciating her beauty as his mind wandered. He wished his grandfather could be there to shower him with compliments and guidance.

It occurred to him that his brother deserved such compliments more than he did. Penelope thanked him and noted his intense gaze on her face, prompting her to question if something was amiss. After placing the milk on the sideboard, she left the bed in her pyjamas and briefly checked her reflection in the mirror, confirming her appearance was fine. Upon returning to the room, she sensed a shift in Christopher's demeaner and felt his intense and lustful gaze upon her. The silence between them stirred something inside her, and she perceived a similar change in Christopher's demeaner.

Penelope, a shrewd and strategic woman in her dealings with men, employed her wit to navigate situations. Struggling to break the silence, she inquired,

"So, what time is it?" Christopher glanced at his wristwatch and responded, *"It's 8:30."*

"I've made up my mind that you should meet my family, and later, I'd like to take you to the gravesite. But before that, we can stop by town for a decent meal. You must be hungry, right?" Christopher queried.

"Yes, I am," Penelope replied.

"As soon as you're ready, we can set off."

After hours of going without proper food, what Penelope yearned for was milk, appreciating Christopher's considerate gesture. However, milk, although a liquid sustenance, couldn't quell the profound hunger she was experiencing. Her appetite was ravenous.

Chapter 19

At precisely 9:30 AM, Christopher and Penelope arrived in town. The streets were already bustling with both vehicle and pedestrian activity, making it a challenge for them to locate a parking spot. Eventually, they managed to find an available space, albeit some distance away from Ocean Basket restaurant. When Christopher inquired about dining preferences, Penelope expressed her desire for seafood.

"Seafood," Christopher echoed, glancing at her. *"Many people believe seafood acts as an aphrodisiac,"* he added, leading to a smile from Penelope.

"I've heard that too, but do you believe in such notions?" Penelope playfully returned the question to Christopher.

"What's your perspective on it?" Christopher countered with a question.

"I haven't really paid much attention to that. Nevertheless, I enjoy it for its nutritional value," Penelope explained.

"That's a valid reason as well," Christopher remarked, sharing a smile with her.

After exchanging glances, they parked their vehicle and retraced their steps, realizing they had passed Ocean Basket Restaurant by about 200 meters. As they walked, their progress was frequently interrupted by Penelope's interest in various items displayed in shop windows. At one point, she even requested to enter a jewellery store, where she admired a pair of earrings. Christopher later discovered her fascination as she asked the shop attendant for a closer look.

"Aren't these beautiful?" Penelope inquired, showcasing the earrings for his approval.

Christopher, unfamiliar with women's interests, quickly had to come up with a response. *"You enjoy them, don't you?"* he managed to say, surprising himself with his balanced and thoughtful answer.

"Absolutely, Christopher. What woman wouldn't?"

Penelope replied, returning the earrings and then shifting her attention to rings displayed in the nearby glass counter. *"Look at these rings, Christopher."*

Eager to accommodate her, Christopher approached the display. Curious about the store, Penelope inquired, *"What's the name of this place?"*

"It's the 'Mel Gibson Passion of Christ Jewellery," the sales lady responded.

When Penelope asked about other jewellery, the attendant pointed to another section of the shop.

Christopher seized the opportunity, saying, "I don't even know what size would fit me." He hoped this would initiate further steps.

"Neither do I," Penelope agreed.

"Why not try some? It's important to know these things beforehand," the attendant encouraged.

"Sure, why not?" Christopher agreed, glad to jump at the chance.

He had anticipated this scenario.

They both tried on several rings, and Christopher paid closer attention to Penelope's ring size than his own. He had examined the earrings and the diamond ring, reassuring himself that he could remember a two-digit figure. "I'm good with numbers; how could I forget a two-digit figure?" Christopher thought.

After spending twenty minutes in the shop, Penelope's hunger became pronounced, and they left to find a restaurant. At the restaurant, she ordered prawns and shrimps, while Christopher opted for oysters and lobsters. Before their main meal, they were served bread, soup, and salads.

"Do you also enjoy seafood?" Penelope inquired.

"Why do you ask?" Christopher responded.

"Your order is quite seafood-heavy," Penelope noted.

"I do, for the same reason as you," Christopher replied, wondering if he might be in denial.

While at the restaurant, Penelope realized she needed to call her friends and update them on her travels and findings. After the meal, she asked Christopher where she could find a pay phone. Fortunately, there was one conveniently placed inside the restaurant, and she purchased a phone card from the counter.

Penelope made a call to Edith, informing her of her safe travel and briefly mentioning that the trip had provided answers to her mysterious dreams. She shared that she was currently in town with the brother from her dreams.

"Where is he?" Edith inquired.

"It's a long story. I'll explain when I see you," Penelope responded. *"I'm about to meet the rest of the family now, so I'll talk to you later."* With that, she hung up the phone.

The call triggered a realization in Penelope's mind – the idea of meeting his family. She pondered over it, wondering why she had gone along with the plan without even asking for his reasons. An hour later, they were on their way, and Penelope's thoughts were consumed by this new revelation. Doubts crept in as she questioned the purpose of meeting his family.

"This is a bad idea," she thought.

She worried about how he would introduce her and whether he would reveal the whole truth. Penelope feared being blamed for the death of their son and brother, even though she had never met him before the tape and photos in his brother's living room, as well as in her dreams.

Troubled, Penelope mustered the courage to ask Christopher, *"So, how is this going to work?"*

"What do you mean?" Christopher asked, seeking clarification.

"What will you tell them about me?" Penelope inquired, her *concern*, evident.

As Christopher heard the tone of Penelope's voice, he noticed the worried expression on her face. Responding to her concern, he said, "*I'm not sure. What would you prefer me to say?*"

"Just avoid mentioning the accident," Penelope requested.

"Why do you want to keep that a secret?" Christopher asked.

"Imagine being in my shoes for a moment, feeling that guilt. Your family might not take it well, and I don't think I can handle any more emotional burden," Penelope explained.

"But you're not responsible for anything, at least not in my eyes," Christopher assured her.

"It's not about you. We can't predict their reaction. 'Something bad happened because of me' – you think they'll be

happy to meet me?" Penelope questioned.

"Alright, I'll handle it. I'll figure out how to approach the situation," Christopher assured her.

As they continued driving, they eventually arrived at a white house. The street was adorned with fallen petals, creating a vibrant scene. They stepped out, and Christopher opened the door for Penelope. Observing their arrival, neighbours seemed curious, and Penelope noticed a sense of watchfulness from various directions.

Juliet, Christopher's mother, greeted them at the door with a warm smile. She hugged Christopher and shook Penelope's hand, leaving a positive impression. Inside, Juliet's excitement was evident, and she even whispered to Christopher that Penelope was cute.

Penelope felt curious about the warm reception, yet she knew she couldn't inquire as a stranger. During the introduction, she was presented as an old friend of the twins who had come to pay her respects to the late family member. Though appreciated, the introduction didn't meet the expectations of Christopher's family.

The Virtues of Split Personality

Later, Christopher and Penelope visited the graveyard. Christopher bought roses – a cream one for himself and a red one for Penelope. As they stood before Christopher's grave, Penelope knelt down and read the engraved inscription which read:

"CHRISTOPHER WRIGHT

SON, GRANDSON AND BROTHER

BORN: SEPTEMBER 8, 1972

DIED: SEPTEMBER 11, 2004

MAY YOUR SOUL REST IN ETERNAL PEACE."

Overwhelmed with emotion, she began to cry, realizing the reality of the situation. Christopher comforted her, and after a few minutes, she stepped back to allow Christopher to place his flowers.

Christopher knelt down, expressing his emotions to his late twin brother. He assured him that Penelope was captivating and that he would cherish and respect her. Their visit concluded in silence as they walked back to the car.

"*You know what? I've just thought that we should also go see this other person,*" Christopher mentioned as they *returned* to the car.

"Who?" Penelope asked.

"*I'd love for it to be a surprise, if you're okay with that,*" Christopher replied.

Though a bit uncertain, Penelope didn't decline the idea. Christopher sensed her apprehension, and as they drove, he occasionally glanced at her, noticing her preoccupation with the upcoming surprise.

As they turned onto a gravel road, memories from a previous day flooded Penelope's mind, briefly choking her. Concerned, Christopher asked if she was alright, and she assured him she was fine, avoiding mentioning the cause of her distress. They continued in silence, and Christopher repeatedly checked on her, finding amusement in her unnecessary worries.

Finally, they reached the end of the road, entering a property where an old man with a bowler hat awaited. Christopher greeted him warmly, and they exchanged greetings. Penelope heard the man inquire if she was the one, and Christopher quickly clarified that she was just a friend. Mr. Wright then welcomed

The Virtues of Split Personality

Penelope with enthusiasm, praising her beauty and playfully suggesting he'd divorce to marry her.

In the living room, Mr. Wright continued to interact with Christopher and Penelope. He shared anecdotes about family relationships and approvals, highlighting the significance of special connections. His wife's presence and subtle response tempered the conversation. Christopher observed that Penelope's presence had likely prevented a potential heated argument between his grandparents.

As the visit unfolded, Penelope's emotions were restrained for the sake of their guest. Christopher recognized that Penelope's presence had defused a potentially tense situation and kept the atmosphere more harmonious.

Christopher couldn't help but imagine the potential escalation and how various issues could have been dragged into the argument that his grandparents were about to engage in.

"Anyway, just like I was saying. Unless there is such a big hindrance, I don't think I'm interested in meeting any other women," Mr. Wright declared, then stood up and left the room.

He added, *"Besides, I've met and only know you,"* directing his last words toward Penelope. Christopher felt a wave of embarrassment and lowered his head, resting his chin on his chest as his grandmother hugged both him and Penelope.

Confused by the interaction, his grandmother asked, *"What was that all about?"*

Christopher, still flustered, shrugged his shoulders. He was more embarrassed now due to his grandfather's puzzling remark.

"Never mind him, he can be so misleading and confusing," his grandmother reassured.

Turning her attention to Penelope, Liz warmly addressed her, *"My dear, it's good to have you around."*

"Thank you," Penelope replied.

Liz shifted her gaze to Christopher, who was lost in thought. She called his name to get his attention.

"Oh, I'm sorry. Yes, Granny," Christopher responded.

Liz subtly gestured toward Penelope, prompting

Christopher to realize that he hadn't properly introduced Penelope to his grandmother. Taking a deep breath, he exhaled and prepared to rectify the oversight.

"Granny, this is my friend, Penelope. She's from Dallas and has come to pay her last respects to Christopher. We were just coming from the grave site, and I thought we could also say hi to you,"
Christopher introduced Penelope, explaining their visit in detail.

"Penelope, it's so nice of you, and we're so grateful," Liz expressed her appreciation.

Turning her attention to Penelope, she asked, *"So, how are you, my dear?"*

"I'm fine, thank you," Penelope replied.

"Please, you're welcome here anytime," Liz warmly invited.

Later that afternoon, as Christopher and Penelope bid farewell to Liz, they exchanged glances upon hearing her shout, "Please visit us more often" from the front doorway. They were uncertain who the appeal was directed at.

As they resumed their journey, Penelope asked Christopher if he had informed his grandfather about their visit. When Christopher confirmed that he hadn't, Penelope expressed how it seemed like Mr. Wright had prior information about their presumed relationship.

"Did that bother you?" Christopher inquired.

"No, but I thought it bothered you," Penelope admitted.

Christopher agreed, *"You're right to think that way. It did sound like he had upfront information. But what can I say? That's my grandfather."*

On their way, Christopher decided to give Penelope a tour of the town before heading home. Later in the evening, they went to a nightclub, enjoying drinks and conversation. However, a guy approached Penelope and asked her to dance, ignoring Christopher.

"Ask him," Penelope suggested, appreciating the attention.

Christopher declined the request, asserting his presence, and stepped away to get more drinks. The same guy approached Penelope again, inquiring about her relationship status.

The Virtues of Split Personality

"Are you seeing him?" he asked, pointing to Christopher.

Penelope responded, *"No, I'm just visiting."*

Explaining his motives, the guy said, *"I thought you should know that he is not a ladies' man. I'm sorry to say this, but how can someone so beautiful be with someone who can't appreciate her as she deserves?"*

Penelope dismissed the guy when she saw Christopher returning to the table, but his words left her pondering. A conclusion formed in her mind that Christopher might be gay, especially considering what she had observed at his parents' home.

As they returned to the flat around midnight, Penelope struggled to muster the courage to address her suspicions. She decided she needed to put Christopher to a test. They slept similarly to the previous night, but Penelope surprised Christopher by waking up on the mattress with him in the morning. He kissed her forehead, but she remained asleep. When she woke up, her immediate thought was about her journey back. Christopher wasn't in the room, so she rushed to the bathroom. Christopher was already up, making breakfast in the kitchen. After getting dressed, Penelope realized she hadn't informed Christopher about her departure. She felt awkward approaching him, fearing it might come across as if he had offended her. Nonetheless, she had to address it and walked to the kitchen.

"Good morning, you're up?" Christopher greeted and asked.

"Yes," Penelope replied.

Christopher was making an effort to engage in conversation, trying not to make her feel embarrassed about sleeping on the floor with him.

"Fine, and by the way, I forgot to tell you, I'll be leaving this morning," Penelope mentioned.

Christopher's silence and expression revealed his surprise and disappointment. *"So soon?"* he asked, processing the news.

"I have to report for work tomorrow," Penelope explained.

Christopher contemplated the situation before suggesting, *"Stay and fly out tomorrow with the 6:00 AM plane. I'll take care of it. You'll have enough time to report at your usual time."*

Concerned, Penelope responded, *"Are you sure about that? Your job must be paying you generously."*

Christopher reflected, *"It's not about that. I think it has more to do* with my emotional investment. While my job pays well, it's not overpaying me."

He assured Penelope, "All we need to do right now is make the reservation."

It turned out that Penelope had no objections to staying longer, hoping that it would provide her the chance to confirm her suspicions. They spent that Sunday morning indoors together and eventually drove out to buy her ticket, deciding to purchase it in the afternoon for added assurance.

That night, they slept together on the bed, honoring the wish that had brought them together. There seemed to be a natural attraction between them, and they held each other close as they slept. Despite the intense connection, they respected the boundaries of their meeting.

In Christopher's arms, Penelope contemplated her own situation and compared it to his. She pondered the reasons behind people's perceptions of him and sought an explanation.

Early the next morning, they both got up and took showers consecutively, with Penelope going first. When she emerged from the shower in his robe, Christopher surprised her by untying the strap, running his finger down her body, and then kissing her gently below her navel. This unexpected act left her momentarily stunned and made her question the depth of the similarities between her dreams and reality.

At the airport, they shared a passionate hug and kissed on the lips before parting ways. Penelope's plane took off at 7:00 AM. They had arranged for Christopher to visit her in two weeks' time over the weekend, a decision driven by the emotional investment they had made in their connection. Before that, Penelope planned to ask Christopher for his photos to show her friends as a way to reassure them upon her return.

Chapter 20

Penelope returned to her hometown around 8:00 AM, providing her ample time to visit her house and prepare for work. When she arrived at her workplace, she assumed her usual persona that everyone recognized. She expressed gratitude to her helpful colleague, who had been resourceful when needed. Following the customary greetings from her colleagues upon returning from her leave, she updated her supervisor and then contacted Edith and Christine to inform them of her comeback.

Later that day, she was the final person to join their meeting spot. Before sitting down, she retrieved a small bundle of money from her handbag and handed it to Edith. With a kiss on the forehead, Penelope expressed her appreciation, saying, *"Thank you very much."*

Understandably, it would have been quite ungrateful for Penelope to reject the money in that manner. Yet, with her friend Edith, Penelope had intended to display a certain demeanor. She approached Christine and hugged her from behind, whispering, *"Thank you, love,"* into her ear. Placing her hands on her hips, Penelope paused, casting a scornful glance at Edith. Edith was taken aback, perceiving Penelope's gesture as a display of attitude.

Curious, Edith inquired, *"What are you up to?"*

Penelope observed Edith's familiar arrogant expression as she posed her question. Christine found herself caught in the situation, shifting her gaze between the two, fully aware of the unfolding dynamics but curious about the outcome. Taking her time, Penelope walked over to Edith and affectionately kissed her on the cheek, saying, *"I love you so much, and I can't imagine what I would have done without you."*

Edith responded with impatience, urging Penelope to cut to the chase. *"Spare me the theatrics and get to the point. You know exactly what we're eager to hear. Sit down and share the details of your trip,"* Edith insisted.

Both Christine and Penelope's lips curled into smiles. Penelope playfully asked, *"What would you like to know?"*

"Don't play games. Ah, I see you're back to reality," Edith remarked.

"Are you being serious?" Penelope sought confirmation.

She pulled out a chair and settled down, noting the anxiety on Edith and Christine's faces. Resting her hands on the armrests, she leaned her head back and let out a sigh. Edith noticed the money still in Penelope's hand and inquired, *"What's this?"*

"It's not that I'm ungrateful, but I flew in this morning, and this is my remaining funds from the trip. Unless you'd like it to become a debt," Penelope explained.

"Not a chance, so when is he arriving?" Edith asked.

"Who?" Penelope countered.

"Come on, Penelope, enough with the games. Get on with it. I'm just as eager to hear your story," Christine chimed in.

"But Christine, who said he's coming? Coming where and why?" Penelope retorted.

"Whatever, just spill the beans," Christine insisted.

"You know he needs to face the consequences of his actions," Edith interjected.

"What do you mean by that?" Penelope questioned.

"He should be accountable for the troubles he's caused and the expenses too, unless you're telling us he's already made amends in some way."

"So, how was he?" Edith inquired, raising her eyebrows and subtly swaying her hips.

"Come on, Edith, didn't I mention there was a sombre aspect to those dreams when I called you?" Penelope reminded her.

"You did," Edith acknowledged.

"That's what you should have been asking me about. 'Why is the sexual aspect so significant to you? Is Richard experiencing some sort of sexual drought?'" Penelope teased.

"I just want to know if this guy has broadened your sexual horizons," Edith replied.

For a moment, Penelope fell silent, her face downturned. When she finally looked up, her previously bright expression had transformed into one of sadness and gloom. "He is dead," she announced, observing the shock on her friends' faces.

"The man from my dreams has passed away," she repeated to ensure they understood correctly.

"What are you saying?" Christine asked, bewildered.

"He was already deceased even before my dreams began. Remember that accident I told you about, the one a few weeks ago?" Penelope inquired, knowing she had previously mentioned it.

The Virtues of Split Personality

"Yes, the one where a small car collided with a truck," Edith clarified, making sure she had the right incident in mind.

"Yes, that was him," Penelope confirmed, recounting the events of the accident. *"Do you recall my last dream where he told me to go to New Orleans?"* she asked her friends.

Christine and Edith both listened intently and responded in unison, *"Yes..."*

"The man I encountered there is his identical twin," Penelope revealed.

As Penelope concluded her account, both Christine and Edith were in tears. They excused themselves and headed to the restroom to compose themselves. Upon their return, Penelope asked, *"Would you like to hear more?"*

"No, I can't handle it anymore," Edith was the first to decline.

"I thought this was the part you were eager to know about," Penelope remarked.

"Whatever," Edith retorted.

"He's visiting next weekend," Penelope informed them.

The Virtues of Split Personality

"The deceased guy?" Edith questioned.

"Come on, you're not paying attention. The guy I encountered," Penelope clarified, prompting laughter from Christine.

"No, no, no. It's hard to keep up with your ghostly romance, it's quite eerie," Edith admitted.

Penelope felt the need to defend herself. She reached into her handbag and pulled out some photos.

"Oh my God, he's handsome," Christine exclaimed as they looked at the photos.

"I've always told you that you were a player. Did you really have to be involved with both of them?" Edith confronted Penelope.

"Leave me alone and just be quiet," Penelope retorted.

"Anyway, I can't blame you. He looks irresistible," Edith conceded.

Christopher and Penelope rarely went a day without talking on the phone. If one didn't call, the other surely did. Soon enough, Christopher's promised visit became a reality. He arrived on a Saturday morning by plane, and Penelope eagerly awaited him at the airport. Her love for him was evident in her anxious, expectant gaze. She was the first to arrive, pacing back and forth even though the plane was on time, as announced in the public announcement.

Eventually, the plane touched down right on schedule. This time, she didn't wait to see him disembark. Instead, she attempted to bypass the public barrier and run towards the exit. Security officers intervened, redirecting her to wait with the other passengers. Overwhelmed, she ran to the glass windows overlooking the runway. A shout escaped her lips when she spotted him walking toward the terminal. As he came into view, she rushed toward him. The applause of onlookers accompanied their emotional reunion, and even the security officers were lenient.

In the foyer, Christopher held Penelope's right hand with his left and playfully made her spin around. Nervously, she complied, her smile revealing her anticipation. He admired her, wanting her more. Her financial status didn't matter to him; Christopher had made up his mind. *"My brother's girlfriend has been more beneficial to me in his death than he ever was in his life,"* he thought, a pang of nostalgia hitting him. *"I miss him, though."*

They headed straight home and later ventured into town. Since Christopher was only visiting for the weekend, Penelope felt obligated to show him around. Before they set out, she called her friends to announce his arrival. Edith and Christine were eager to meet him and decided to join them at their usual meeting spot.

Edith and Christine arrived at the meeting place before Penelope and Christopher. The wait felt endless, and Christine alerted Edith when she finally spotted the approaching couple. As they neared the table, Christopher noticed the two ladies with wide smiles. He glanced at Penelope, who was equally beaming. Holding hands, they approached the table, sensing that something significant was unfolding.

Once they reached the table, Edith and Catherine offered them chairs. Penelope introduced Christopher, then excused herself to use the restroom. Edith followed suit as Penelope disappeared around the corner.

Inside the restroom, Edith couldn't contain her excitement and let out a scream, startling Penelope. *"Yes, girl, he really is cute, just like in his photos,"* Edith exclaimed.

"Yes, Edith, and he's all mine," Penelope replied.

"Go girl!" Edith cheered, and they shared a joyful laugh and hug.

The Virtues of Split Personality

Penelope and Christopher enjoyed another seafood meal, followed by an intimate evening. Throughout their lovemaking, Penelope shed tears, which made Christopher feel a sense of pride and accomplishment. However, her tears were a result of the emotional realization that she was finally connecting with her true love.

The following morning, Christopher woke up before Penelope and went to the kitchen to prepare breakfast. He wanted to surprise her with breakfast in bed. Soon after, Penelope woke up and realized he was missing. Confused, she almost uttered her thoughts aloud, but only her lips moved.

Suddenly, she heard the sound of running tap water and caught a whiff of something delicious cooking. With the half-closed door and a sense of anticipation, she cautiously left the bed and made her way to the kitchen. At the kitchen entrance, she peeked in, then instinctively pulled back, hands clutching her chest. She closed her eyes briefly and let out a relieved sigh. Gathering her courage, she approached him from behind and embraced him. *"I love you so much,"* she whispered. Christopher was slightly startled but managed to compose himself. He turned around and planted a kiss on her lips. *"Good morning. You're awake. My surprise is ruined now,"* he teased.

"What surprise?" Penelope inquired.

"Breakfast in bed," Christopher responded.

"No, no, no," Penelope protested before playfully darting back to the bedroom.

Christopher flew back on Monday morning, but their communication remained consistent through phone calls, and they took turns visiting each other at regular intervals.

Patson M. Chifumbe

The Virtues of Split Personality